ABOUT THE

Arthur Allwright began his writing career at the age of seventy. At the insistence of his grandchildren, he produced his first striking work, answering their question, "What was it like, being an evacuee during the Second World War?" "A Stranger And Afraid" tells subsequent generations what it was like to be an eight- year-old stranger in an even stranger land for three years with a Quaker family in Somerset. You should make time to read that book!

The publication of the book inspired him to join a Kent-based group of writers, who turned his interests to short story writing and poetry. He enjoys sharing his experiences and stories with school groups and communities. The natural progression is to share some of his work with you.

To add interest for the reader, the author introduces each story with the background, explaining why the story was written.

By the same author

A STRANGER AND AFRAID
(A true story of the author's wartime evacuation)

ISBN 1-904224-31-8

TIME FOR A QUICKIE

(SHORT STORIES FOR BUSY PEOPLE)

By Arthur Allwright

Best Wishes.

Arthur Allwright.

2009.

Copyright page

First published in 2008 by YouWriteOn.com
Copyright Text Arthur Allwright

First Edition

The author asserts the moral right under the Copyright, Designs and Patents Act 1988 to be identified as the author of this work.

All rights reserved. No part of this publication may be reproduced, stored in a retrieval system, or transmitted, in any form or by any means without the prior written consent of the author, nor be otherwise circulated in any form of binding or cover other than that in which it is published and without a similar condition being imposed on the subsequent purchaser.

Published by YouWriteOn.com

INDEX

THE AGE OF FEAR	1
A STICKY T'DO	17
THE ACADEMY OF CHANCE	23
LOVE AND MARRIAGE	31
LOVE AND THE STARS	33
THE PEAR TREE	43
THE MEASURE OF LOVE	51
THE SECRET ROOM	55
ST. VALENTINE'S DAY	61
THE LUCK OF GEORGE	65
I'M DYING TODAY	95
NOCTURNAL HAPPINESS	99
THE CARNAGE THAT WAS CULLODEN	109
FORGOTTEN HELL	117
WAITING FOR THE "OFF"	127
CATS	129
LOVE MATCH	137
FREE FROM FEAR	145
THE HAUNTED HEAVEN	151
HONOUR RESTORED	161
WEAPON OF MASS DESTRUCTION	171

INTRODUCTION

It happens to all of us. We think that our day is fully mapped out, when suddenly, there is a pause. Not long enough to bring forward another chore. Certainly, turning on the tele would defeat our plans. We daren't get embroiled in a phone conversation and, if you are like me, remembering how to text a friend would involve finding and reading The Manual.

Something like twenty minutes becomes available and we have the opportunity to sink into that DFS corner-piece. No, this is not the time to wonder when shall we have finished paying for the furniture. It is time to relax. Our partner could be checking the Cheltenham selections in the smallest room, or the baby needn't be wakened for half an hour.

The four hundred page novel that we started reading recently requires too long to recapture the plot. We daren't close our eyes. We need a few moments of relaxed enjoyment. If only we possessed a pocket entertainer. Look no further .... as you turn these pages, the answer will be in your own hands. Obviously, the stories were written with you in mind.

THE AGE OF FEAR

Let's start at the beginning. This was my first project set by a Kent group of budding authors. We were challenged to write a 5000 word story, written in the 1st person singular relating to a true experience of the author. The choice of subject was not a problem; I just relived that awful day in 1944 when, at the age of thirteen …………..Well, why not read about it?

The story was entered for an on-line world-wide short story competition, receiving a Top-Ten "Highly Commended" award out of the 577 entries submitted. The subsequent stories were the result of that springboard.

THE AGE OF FEAR

My God! There was no mistaking the stuttering, echoing drone in the sky. Fear tightened my stomach muscles and the pounding of my heartbeat vibrated throughout my body. It was another of those revenge weapons, unmanned winged rockets with a deadly explosive nose fired by the desperate Germans from mobile launching pads in Picardy and propelled over the English Channel by pulse-jet engines..

My next door neighbour Bernard and I ran into the garden knowing that thousands of pairs of eyes would have already watched the path of this killer with the fiery ejection from its tail. Now it was our turn to urge it on to somebody else's patch. Not here please.

We knew that the first line of defence against these robots was over the English Channel where our fighter pilots demonstrated their skills by flying alongside the low-flying "doodlebugs" as they had been christened and tried to tilt them over with their wing tips to redirect them into the sea. The second line was the ack-ack fire along the Kent coast, followed by a network of barrage balloons, whose cables occasionally tripped an intruder. But this one, like most of its fellows had pierced the haphazard defence and would continue an uncontrolled journey until its fuel expired, leaving the winged bomb to glide into whatever helpless mass happened to be below.

We stood on the Anderson shelter to give us that extra six feet of height to get a better view over the elm trees at the bottom of the garden.

"It's missed us," he announced knowingly and as if to tempt fate, he added, "I'd hate to be near the bang if it hit the gasometer."

It was the sort of nervous conversation prompted by fear. My reply was stymied by the sudden silence. The engine had cut out and the nose dipped slightly. Desperate voices in adjoining gardens conjectured about the likely point of impact.

"Looks towards Epsom or Cheam"

"More like Worcester Park, it's changed course a bit," corrected another.

The gliding took an eternity. Twenty or thirty seconds is forever when you think that your life is on the line. The inevitable bang came, followed by the tell-tale evidence from the billowing funnel of white, then black smoke, that the possible spot of impact was nearer than expected, possibly only two miles away. Relief from fear shows itself in different ways.

"Poor devils," came a cry a few doors along the gardens of our terraced houses, aimed at the unknown ordinary people who had paid the price of being in the wrong place at the wrong time.

"Let's have a cuppa," called another.

Bernard had a better idea and within minutes, still in our school clothes, we were on our bikes, heading in the direction of the smoke. Both of our Mums were out at First Aid lessons and Dads would not be home from work for a couple of hours and this was exciting for two lads of thirteen. A rattling loose rear mudguard and soft tyres made peddling my bike hard going but I was being driven on by Bernard's better display on his well-maintained Raleigh. This was our third attempt to chase a doodle bug but each of the two previous ones was further away than we had presumed. We were convinced, however, that this time would be different and the closeness of the rising plumes of grey smoke, unfolding against a clear blue September afternoon sky, spurred us on. The uneven railway crossing threatened to shake my bike to pieces and as we tackled the long strength-sapping gradient that followed, the additional strain began to take its toll on my wonky pedals which creaked, gasping for oil.

Two army ambulances overtook us and screeched round a corner, indicating the route that we should take. We followed with increasing speed, sensing that we were not far from our goal. The first signs of damage were lumps of roof tiles littering the road and at about the same time, people were outside their homes gaping at the broken windows. Nobody seemed to be doing anything, just gaping. At the next junction a broken road sign, "Ruxley Lane" hanging limply, gave the introduction to the extent of the carnage wrought by that single intruder. Amidst the smoking arena of war, two tree-lined roads of beautifully maintained houses of the 1930 era had been rudely laid to waste. The mortgaged castles of so many families were no more. Furniture and clothes festooned the remaining trees. Two jets of flames illuminated the path of fractured gas pipes and a three legged dog hobbled past us, howling in pain.

Bernard clutched his stomach and heaved as if he was about to be sick, turned his bike round and pointed in a homeward direction.

"Come on," he gasped, "this is no place for us. We shouldn't have come."

Nothing more was said. We half walked, half peddled along the rural back lanes of Worcester Park. The bravado of our ill-advised trek had been extinguished by the unbelievable extent and stench of the destruction. Prior to today, we had coped with the damage of individual bombs, or sticks of bombs, even close to our own homes. We openly admitted that during lulls in air raids, we had secretly wished for the danger to return, even though in the reality of an air raid, we sweated with terror at the sound of approaching bombers.

Our silent thoughts were suddenly exploded by yet another torch of death in the sky, getting louder and louder. In a split second, the two of us realised we were still in the middle of a raid and we wished that we were anywhere but here.

At about 5,000 ft, the doodle bug was still full of energy but to our horror, it turned out to be one of those rockets that dipped without warning and gathered speed in a straight line with its engine at full power and it was aiming directly at us.

"Christ," screamed Bernard, "let's get to the other side of the railway bridge."

Standing on our peddles and finding unknown strength, driven by fear, we raced through the arch, bounced up the tarred pavement and into a dried up ditch beside a hedge. As the tangled mess of two boys and bikes hit the ditch, a man threw himself across our bodies, yelling at us to keep our heads down. His words were obliterated by a crescendo of ear-rending proportions. The earth literally shook relentlessly with a series of explosions.

"Keep your heads down." We needed no telling. I felt a jab on the back of my leg and could feel and hear chunks of debris falling around us. I found that I had been holding my breath for the whole duration of the episode, just as I had when I was anticipating pain in the dentist's chair the previous week. As the cacophony of sound diluted, there was a gradual movement amongst us. The old man who had shielded us with his body, extricated himself, stood up and shook himself like a chicken after it had enjoyed a dust bath. As I disentangled my leg from the bike frame, I was aware of the sudden silence amid the dense smoke and an obnoxious smell permeating the foggy air. It was a memory that would stay with me for ever. My legs had turned to jelly. Both of us were shaking and the old man was walking aimlessly in the middle of the road.

"We're alive," I said, not convincing myself that it was true.

"Are we? I can't hear anything except a ringing in my ears."

A glance around us left us bemused. In spite of the enormity of the explosion, we could see no damage on our side of the railway embankment, except for a few broken branches of trees. Without realising it, Bernard's shout to get through the arch had undoubtedly saved our lives. The high railway embankment had protected us from the direct blast of the impact, centred on the Plough pub a hundred yards on the other side of the bridge.

"We had better get home before anyone knows we're missing." urged Bernard as we wheeled our bikes along the pavement.

With a trickle of blood meandering down to my socks I tried to get on my bike, but the combination of a bent wheel and my jittery legs made it impossible. It was as much as I could do, to walk at all. Bernard, however was intent on getting home and made it obvious. Eventually, he made the excuse of wanting to pee and said that he would dash home and tell our mums if they were home, that we were OK.

My stomach ached, my head vibrated with every step and I began to sweat with the difficulty of dragging the injured bike. A pigeon suddenly chose the moment that I was passing beneath a tall tree, to add his contribution to my shattered nerves, by flapping his wings in a desperate attempt to escape from a pair of marauding magpies. For a brief second, I visualised another doodle bug and I chastised myself for reacting so negatively and causing my heart to race unnecessarily. I was on edge, without doubt, but I told myself that I needed to get a grip.

The local school loomed and my own need for a pee steered me into the yard and through the "Boys" door. The relief of a never ending pee played a duel role and on my exit I began to think more clearly. As if by magic, there on the school wall was the recent Notice inviting parents to take advantage of pending evacuation opportunities. I used the pencil hanging from the board to add my name and address to the list of about thirty names.

My instinctive action excited me for the homeward journey and my thoughts became centred on the possible reaction at home when I told them of my plan. The focal point in my mind was to avoid a repeat of the afternoon's scare but I suddenly saw the wonderful opportunity of at last finding an excuse to put distance between me and my three sisters with whom I had been engaged in a continuous war, making life at home sheer bedlam.

But events took a different turn when I got home. Everyone was too concerned with other things to be bothered with my arrival and the evening passed without me disclosing my news. Two days later, the matter came to a head when a teacher visited the house to make arrangements for my departure on the Saturday. The quivering lip of mum told its own story and her immediate response was to say that the two younger sisters would have to go as well. By the time the teacher had left, my mother had volunteered to accompany the party of children as one of the helpers. My plans were in shreds.

"Wait till your father gets in," she chastised, "thought you could get away without telling us did you?"

The double-decker London bus, full of local children approached St. Pancras Station. The journey had been a mixture of half hearted singing and outright sobbing. There had been a tearful departure at the school amidst a consoling assurance that the war couldn't go on for much longer. It was the 'not-knowing' that most children feared. How far were we going? Who would be our guardians? When would we see our mums again?

My own thoughts were spoken aloud to my friend, Ivor.

"How can we get on the train without my sisters?"

"Leave it to me," he said, confidently, "just follow me."

So that is what happened. He lead and I followed. The platform was crowded by the time the red bus disgorged its hesitant, unhappy band of forlorn victims. All were bedecked in a mixture of uniforms and ill-fitting clothes and all labelled with a name tag and carrying the regulation brown cardboard box housing the smelly repugnant gasmask.

Walking at speed, we soon left behind the crocodile line from our bus and weaved in and out of groups huddled against the edge of the platform awaiting the arrival of a train.

"Here, put this on," said Ivor, handing me a crumpled black cap from his pocket, "and don't talk to anyone."

We had parked on the edge of a smart bunch of well-dressed boys, all sporting black caps. So that was what Ivor had been searching for. We were now fellow pupils of a posh school and hidden from view of our own group. Luck was on our side because almost immediately, a labouring dirty green engine emitting thick black smoke drew alongside the platform. The noise of whistles, shouting and general excitement was almost drowned by the engine's own input of letting off its excess steam, showering the unfortunate parties that had chosen that spot to stand. Within seconds the whole platform was shrouded in a foggy, smelly dampness.

Doors of the brown carriages were sticky and difficult to open. Some seemed to be locked. But eventually, the entire group at our point had pushed and shoved its way onto the train making for the corridors, ignoring the uninviting hard seats in the compartments. Nobody appeared to count the occupants and Ivor observed that we were safe. This obviously tempted fate and the air was filled with the wailing of the air raid sirens to herald the likely approach of more doodle bugs. The result was immediate and amid a stream of whistles and arm-waving of the railway officials on the platform, the engine gave a sharp "Peep" and our carriage lurched forward, backward and forward again, shaking us unceremoniously. The engine eventually won the battle against the weight of the train and we ere soon making progress through the city, smoke billowing past the window. For most of the evacuees, this was the first train ride that they had experienced and the excitement raised the morale of the cargo.

After the initial excitement, we settled down, gradually being bored by the repetitive nature of the scenery. Occasionally, a boy would raise the tempo of the talking by pointing out aircraft gun sites or barrage balloons festooning the countryside, but the general atmosphere became more subdued and satisfying the "inner man" was a priority. My beetroot sandwiches disappeared in double quick time as did the two fairy cakes made without fat by mum the previous day. Although tasteless, they satisfied a need.

The rocking of the train sent many into the land of Nod, until, after about three hours of stopping and starting, the train braked with unexpected severity. The opening and slamming of doors, accompanied by an escalation in the noise of chattering children announced the arrival at our destination, but almost immediately, a teacher told us to remain where we were because our end of the train would be going on to another station. I sheepishly pushed past a boy with an open window and gazed down the platform, not daring to lean out too far, for fear of being seen. Sure enough, to my delight, I could see my two sisters already alighted, flanked by helpers, including my mother who seemed completely unaware or interested that I was not there. She was probably unprepared for some of us to remain on the train.

"Quick," I beckoned to Ivor, "quick, let's get into the lav in case we're seen."

We stood in the unlit tiny room that smelt of the result of many bad aims by boys who had been thrown around whilst performing. But we were rescued by the departure of the train without any mishap. The plan had worked but suddenly I felt alone and afraid. I had been concentrating on severing myself from my sisters, for several days, but hadn't thought through the consequences. Now, Ivor was my only friend with a great unknown in front of me.

No sooner had the train got up speed, it started to slow down and came to an unexpected stop. We had arrived at our destination. Doors were flung open and we were reminded, loudly, not to leave anything behind and ushered onto the platform, where we found out that all of the other boys were from the same school. Ivor and I were interlopers. Nobody seemed to notice and we were soon on our way by bus through a large town, arriving shortly at a small hall nestling beside a square towered church.

We were met by three bossy looking ladies, who urged us to hurry to a table ladened with food.

"Two sandwiches each, one cake and a drink," called the tallest of the three. "I've heard all about you London boys, greedy. There's a war on and we're short of food. Goodness knows how we shall be able to cope with you all coming to our town at short notice."

Not only were they bossy, but also bad tempered.

"And don't make a mess. Use the plates provided."

Ivor and I looked at each other. He had lost his sparkle and sat quietly staring at his empty plate.

"Come on, let's go onto the stage away from the school and play Dabs" I suggested.

Without saying a word he hoisted himself onto the black splintery stage and took the precious five stones from his pocket. We played silently for at least half an hour, during which time the hall seemed to be losing its inmates. Suddenly, bossy lady approached us demanding to know our names and asking us why we had not gone out with the other boys.

"Everyone has been accounted for and all the homes have been allocated with one or two boys. Why aren't you on the list? You are from Rutlish School aren't you?"

"No"

"What are we going to do?" And after a pause that seemed to be an eternity, she continued, "pick up your things. We shall have to walk round the streets until we find someone who will have you. But goodness knows why they should bother with you two."

I was now too tired to bother as well. All I wanted to do was to have more to eat and go to sleep. We dragged behind the lady who was armed with a fat wad of papers. She occasionally stopped at a gateway, consulted her notes and then walked away, quickening her pace and leaving us further behind.

"We'll try here. Smarten yourselves up and straighten your ties. You both look so untidy."

She gave three sharp knocks and told us to take our hands out of our pockets. An elderly lady opened the door slightly and immediately slammed it shut. We could hear her shouting from behind the door, telling the lady to take the boys away. I gave a sigh of relief. Four doors further on we stopped again and went through the same ritual. This time much younger lady answered the door and although she had a boy of her own, she didn't want another and wished us a happy stay in Heanor. "So that's the name of the place, I thought."

Two more houses in the same street brought further rebuffs and at one of them, where our lady was more persistent, the owner man had a blackened face, just as if he had been up the chimney. He got cross and called his dog, a fierce Alsatian, nearly as big as me and he threatened to let go of his collar if we didn't go. Both Ivor and I raced out of the garden and into the road. Our lady wasn't far behind but we noticed that she was getting increasingly agitated with each refusal.

With my legs weakening at each step, I finally stopped and sat on a wall, rubbing my eyes. I was already questioning my cowardly decision to leave home and come to this place where nobody wanted me. With one exception all of the houses at which we had called, were old people and I wouldn't want to stay with them. Ivor then voiced my own wish.

"I want to go home. I'm hungry and tired. I want to go home. No one wants us."

The lady came over to us and seemed to be a different person.

"I'm sorry, boys. I hadn't realised that you were so tired. You've had a long day, but I don't know why you weren't on the list. But I don't know what to do. We are getting nowhere knocking on these doors. Let's go back to the hall and I'll contact the Minister."

With renewed strength, we turned and set off for the hall but as we turned the corner away from our unwelcome road, a short grandmotherly lady came puffing up the hill towards us. Recognising the lady guide, she slowed down, patted her aching stomach and called out in a loud excited voice.

"Mrs. Webster, Mrs. Webster, have you got any left? Joe says that we can have one. Am I too late?"

A twinkle in her eye gave me the assurance that this lovely lady was looking for an evacuee. I was already willing her to choose me. She reminded me of my grandmother, always smiling and able to cook lovely bread pudding. She had obviously come out in a hurry. Her hair was dishevelled and she had forgotten to take off her floral apron.

"Hello Mrs. Foulkes," replied our Mrs. Webster, relieved at meeting a positive person at last. "Yes you could say that you are just in time to take these last two lovely boys off my hands. I was beginning to think that they would have to go to the Council estate if nobody wanted them up here. They look good ones," she lied and smoothed my hair to improve the sight. I couldn't help it if I hadn't had a wash all day. I never washed twice at home and the train engine was really smoky.

"I don't know about that, Joe only mentioned having one. Ivor suddenly found his tongue.

"We could sleep together and we promise that we wouldn't talk in bed." Both the ladies laughed but a frown returned to Mrs. Foulkes.

"Alright, I'll take a chance, but I may have to return one of them if Joe says 'No'. Come on home. What's your names?"

It was at this point that I realised that people round here spoke a different language and I could hardly understand what they were saying. Mrs. Foulkes talked non stop for the whole ten minutes of the journey to 17a Watkinson Street, her home. We learnt that Joe was a miner and would be back from the pit in half an hour. He would need a bath and when we had cleared that away, we could have tea, most likely dripping toast and a cake that she had made that morning. Heanor was the name of the town and the place where the train had stopped earlier, was another part of Heanor, called Langley Mill. She had heard that a lot of evacuees would be billeted between the two places.

Number 17a was a terraced house with four steps leading to the front door that was already open. Although it was still daylight, the inside hall was dark and uninviting.

"Leave your things in the passage and come and sit in the dining room. I'll make tea because Joe will want some as soon as he gets in. Take your coat off Ivor and you can help me with the cups. I hope that Joe is in a good mood. I don't know what he'll say."

We didn't have long to wait. The front door had been left ajar and the wafting smell of pipe tobacco announced the arrival of Joe, his heavy boots making a frightening impression on the lino in the hall. The short, black-faced man with a beaming smile edged into the room and looked around.

"Well, what a t'do. What have we here? Art 'em vacees? I didn't expect the whole trainload! Is there a war on, or something?"

Mrs. Foulkes laughed to humour him, but we remained silent because we could only just understand what he was saying.

"They were the only two left at the church and I couldn't leave one on his own, could I?"

"Nay, lass, you'm done the right thing. Now while I drink a nice cuppa, you tell me your names, then you can wash my back"

Being even more confused, Ivor and I sheepishly gave our names and answered his interrogation as conservatively as possible. Then came the shock. Mrs. Foulkes entered the room with a large tin bath and placed it on the rug in front of the smouldering fire that I hadn't even noticed. On her return she brought a hosepipe just like my dad's at home and gave it to me.

"Hold that Arthur and I'll turn on the kitchen tap. Make sure you aim straight. The floor will get wet enough when Joe gets in."

Sure enough, to our amazement, Joe undressed completely in front of us and stood waiting for his bath to be ready. As I sprayed luke warm water into the noisy galvanised tub, Mrs. Foulkes brought in several saucepans full of boiling water to get the right temperature. It was only when Joe eventually lowered himself into the tub, that I noticed the series of gashes and scars all over his body. Ivor was first to comment on them, asking Joe whether he had been fighting.

"Nay, lad," he mused, "it's just what to expect when you work in the pit. Bits of rock fall on you to keep you company."

Mrs.Foulkes then explained that the "pit" was the coal mine where Joe worked and that the coal seams sometimes were only a few feet high and the miners had to crawl to pickaxe the coal from the rock. As they moved forward, they had to shore up the roof to try and prevent the roof from falling on them. He always came home damaged like this.

"I bet you swore when that big gash happened," said Ivor as he dabbed a particularly large blood-soaked swelling with the tattered flannel.

"Nay, I never swear, what's the use? It still hurts if you swear, so why swear?"

The logic went over my head. I was still getting over the fact that I was watching a man have a bath in the dining room. As the dabbing of the wounds continued, Joe reached for his pipe that he had secreted by the tub and lit it, sending whirls of smoke to mingle with the steam from the water. My contribution was minimal in all this activity but I was already hoping that we could stay here. This must be a happy home.

"Can they stay, Joe?"

"Aye, lass, give 'em a go. We can do with a bit of brass. They look good to me, but they'll have to sleep together and they'll have to muck in with the sharing of the housework."

Mrs. Foulkes was true to her word and as soon as Joe had dressed and helped her to carry the tub into the garden, we wiped the floor lino and laid the table for tea. Joe was interested why we had come away when the war was so nearly over. I told him about the doodle bugs and my close shave earlier in the week and he just laughed and said that nothing ever happens in Heanor. Recounting the story sent a shiver down my spine and I lost my tongue for the rest of the evening. Mrs. Foulkes cheered us up a bit when she recalled that their next door neighbour was expecting to have two evacuees, but they hadn't arrived yet.

Sleep came easily and early, but the distance from the war activities meant that Joe didn't bother with blackout curtains and although I had slept soundly, I woke early, realising that for the first time in years, the bright daylight had woken me. I lay for ages, reliving my ordeal that wouldn't let go. But I was safe here and so far, I was happy. My ploy to avoid my sisters gave me great satisfaction and I relished the thought that I would have several months of peace. I awoke to find that my mother had been enquiring about me and Mrs. Foulkes had promised her that she would make sure I wrote home regularly.

Ivor was a laugh and I felt that together, we could enjoy living here. School might be a problem, but nobody would bully me whilst Ivor was around. Yes, things were looking good!

But the school problem was greater than expected and the local Grammar School was full and unable to take us. The only alternative was to hop over the wall at the bottom of Joe's garden and attend the Primary School. After two days I was befriended by one of the teachers and became her assistant, helping her to mark the exercise books of the younger pupils. That was the extent of schooling I received for my seven months stay in Heanor.

After four weeks, Ivor returned home after upsetting Mrs. Foulkes. We were playing cricket in the small garden, when the floor mop that we were using as a bat, broke, and the head described a gentle arc and smashed through the kitchen window. I remained alone for the next six months idling my time away, going to the billiard hall in the High Street most afternoons.

Suddenly, on May 8th at 3pm, Mrs Foulkes called me into the living room where the wireless was blaring out louder than I had ever heard it.

"Listen to this, luv." It was Winston Churchill broadcasting from 10 Downing Street, announcing the end of the War in Europe but reminding us that the war against Japan had not yet been achieved. Everything became a blur. We were both crying, probably for different reasons, but I remember the strange feeling of really wanting to go home as fast as possible; back to the home that I had been pleased to leave seven months earlier.

The all-clear sirens sounded and we found ourselves rushing into the street and linking arms with neighbours and strangers, all singing and crying together.

"Well, I don't suppose we shall be seeing much of you, now." They were the final words of Joe as I left Heanor. Sadly, they proved to be correct.

16

A STICKY T'DO

I have a friend, Ben, in the village who tells a good yarn over a pint. His father–in-law has a villa in France and this is often purloined by Ben's family for a summer break. One such holiday nearly saw the demise of a happy marriage.

The Writers Group to which I belong, often selects a topic for a new story by specifying the opening line. "The Wall Felt Sticky Beneath The Palm Of My Hand" gave me the opportunity of telling you about Ben's narrow escape a few years ago. I have to admit that, although the basis of the story is true, slight exaggerations may have crept in. Call it Writer's License if you like!

A STICKY T'DO

The wall felt sticky beneath the palm of my hand ... not really sticky, like honey, but definitely enough to discolour the rag stone surrounding the fire hearth.

"There," said Michelle, my wife, "you wouldn't believe me yesterday, would you? What can it be?"

It was only the third day of a two month stay at my father-in-law's French retreat near Chinon. As a DIY addict I would make a good snooker player and anything that resembled a house job put prickles on the back of my neck.

"Let's wait and see what it's like tomorrow," I offered and in an attempt to change the subject, "I bet we look funny from behind, two grown-ups with their bums in the air, staring up a chimney." And we laughed, well, we were on holiday and our eighteen month boy, Charles, was asleep in his room upstairs. We fell sideways in a bout of giggling and agreed that it could wait until tomorrow.

Tomorrow arrived and Michelle's bum in the fireplace told its own story.

"No, you can't get out of it this time, there's something wrong. I'll leave it to you to come up with a solution. Not the solution that's trickling down the hearth."

She was right. I poked it with my finger and smelt it. The odour was familiar but it was in the wrong environment. I swiped at a nuisance fly that buzzed around my ear. Then there were two. But wait a minute, the flies were bees and that gave away the cause of the problem. There must be a bee's nest in the chimney. Why hadn't I thought of that possibility before Michele had made an issue of it ?

"What are you doing with that ladder?" came the call from the kitchen window from whence a strong aroma of coffee permeated the early morning air.

"I thought I'd have breakfast on the roof and get on top of the problem. Ha ha" But Michelle was not amused.

I negotiated the comparative safety of the flat roof over the lounge, dragging the step-ladder up behind me and propped it against the chimney breast.

"Bonjour, est-qu'il y a un problem, monsieur?" It was the amiable Pierre from next door

"Peut etre" I replied, confidently and then my French ran out. "Perhaps a bee's nest in the chimney."

The patio door opened with a flourish and into the sunshine stepped the lovely, blonde, buxom partner of Pierre who had greeted us upon our arrival on Saturday with a bottle of Chinon Rouge from their own vineyard.

"Pierre, mon cheri, speak to monsieur Ben in English. How can 'e explain if you gabble away in French? I'm sorry Ben." Rolande smiled upwards, as I smiled downwards, down to where her bra-less serenity had already seen the sun that morning.

"I think that we have a bee's nest in the chimney," I repeated, trying to cut Pierre out of the conversation. "Honey is already trickling down into the fire grate."

"Pas de problem," she confided, "we had the same experience last summer, but my Pierre was very brave and in no time, they had all gone."

I wondered how long I dared to carry on this conversation from this height, recognising that Roland was in no doubt about the attraction to me from my vantage spot. Having moved into my side of the joint garden she sidled seductively closer to the lounge.

"Come on down and we can all discus the solution over some coffee and Calvados. Pierre, fetch the cafetiere et calvados. Michelle," she called, "come and join us."

Although we had been at the villa for only a few days, we were in no doubt about the strength of the French hospitality. "Votre Sante" followed several times whilst Pierre and Rolande between them, explained the plan. They had learned of this extermination procedure from a local builder and the solution was simple. Pierre would go onto the roof and pour petrol down the chimney pot. It was as easy as that! The bees had an aversion to petrol and would evacuate immediately and would never return.

Pierre was as good as his word and by lunchtime, the deed was done and that should have been the end of the story. Unfortunately, nobody had told the bees about the plan and an increasing number of them pestered us in the garden and the lounge.

"No problem," announced Pierre and he proceeded to mount the roof and pour a second dose down the pot.

The atmosphere in the lounge that evening was, to say the least, tense. Michelle had not been too happy about the idea and the honey, however tainted, was running freely into the hearth. An old towel was positioned to absorb the bulk of the sticky mess but further cloths were added when we went to bed. The silence in the bedroom, even after the light had been extinguished for at least an hour, left me in no doubt that all was not well. No "good night" kiss, no cuddle and not even an occasional turn-over to get comfy, told me that Michelle was laying awake, fretting, waiting for the right moment to pounce. Although the chimney breast was in the child's room next to ours, I could smell the odious petrol stench.

I was determined to outlast Michelle in the sleep stakes, hoping that she would eventually drop off, but at 2am I realised that I had dosed off and my bed mate had gone. Something had to be done and lying in bed was not the answer. Without knowing what I was going to do, I slipped out of bed and fought my way through the fumes to the lounge. Poor Michelle. She had been here for over an hour trying to stem the flow of the sticky morass which lapped over the fender and encroached onto the panelled floor. Now, she had sunk onto the sofa, in despair and was sobbing her heart out. Taking her into my arms, I poured out my heart about how sorry I was, that I hadn't saved her from this mess.

"It will be alright, I promise you. You've had enough for tonight. Go back to bed and I'll get it sorted out."

Tiredness and extreme stress had taken its toll, or else Michelle wouldn't have retreated to the bedroom so easily. I covered her lovingly with the duvet, kissed her forehead and left the room. Returning to the lounge I opened the patio doors in an attempt to ventilate the room. At least this was a start and I went into the garden and stared at the chimney. Daylight had crept up on the sleepy pair of villas and the first rays of a new sun were peeping over the horizon.

"Bon matin, you cannot sleep either." It was Pierre in some ill-fitting pyjamas and a mug of coffee. "I can smell your problem," he added, "we must go to plan B. Give me a moment and I shall be with you."

If only I had the courage to dissuade him! But in a situation like this and not having an alternative solution, I stood defenceless in my pyjam trousers. In minutes, he arrived, muttering to himself and brushed past me as if I didn't exist and entered the lounge. Glancing round the garden door, I suddenly realised what the French idiot was going to do.

"This will clear ze problem, stand clear, ……….."

His sentence was never finished. There was an almighty explosion and several minor rumbles as Pierre was thrown savagely through the patio door, landing in a crumpled heap at my feet. Several seconds of silence followed, ended by a horrendous scream from Michelle and a "Sacre Bleu" from Rolande.

"Ben, you've killed my child, you've killed him," she screeched, "Oh God."

Rushing indoors and falling over a heap of rubble, I made a dash for the baby's room upstairs. The devastation was unbelievable. A large hole had replaced the chimney breast and Michelle was desperately clawing at a heap of masonry in the corner where the cot had been. In the semi darkness, I suddenly noticed that the cot, miraculously, had been thrown across the room where the curtains had protected the poor baby who was still asleep. Instinctively, Michelle grabbed Charles and ran screaming downstairs. Rolande had already established that Pierre had sustained no more than a burnt hand and caught Michelle as she staggered uncontrollably into the garden, in a state of extreme shock and steered her into Rolande's home. Pierre and I followed, both obviously suffering, not only mild shock, but from a severe loss of egoistic pride. Neither of us spoke for ages. The ladies did all the talking and it was their plans that dictated the fate of our holiday and the manner in which Pierre would rebuild all the damaged parts of father-in-law's villa.

The open fire was never replaced and to this day honey has been banned.

THE ACADEMY OF CHANCE

Artists, writers and composers have one thing in common. They all express their emotions using their own medium, either with music, paint or words. On my retirement, I found the similarity in two of our hobbies: my wife paints and draws whilst I write. Neither of us sings! The Royal Academy gives me the opportunity of renewing her "Friends of the Academy" annual membership as a Christmas present and to share her pleasure during our trips to London.

During one such visit, after a tiring slow walk around five of the Exhibition Rooms, I succumbed to the temptation of a comfortable sofa from where I could see several pictures. By the time we had left the Academy the seeds of a story had been sown.

THE ACADEMY OF CHANCE

The deep cushioned sofa readily accepted my bulk as I sank thankfully into its alluring frame. Strategically positioned in the centre of Room Seven of The Royal Academy, it beckoned those of senior age who had probably spent an hour or more dutifully studying the details of the exhibits in the previous six rooms. On entering rooms one, two and three, I had read the introductions on plaques at each entrance, enabling me, almost, to understand the pictures that I was about to witness. By room five I had grasped the likely contents and began avoiding the jostling throngs who were intent on getting close enough to count the brush strokes in the dress of the model for "The Wealth of the World". My knees and lower back were telling me to ease off and I found a secluded spot by a doorway and performed two hurried bending exercises, much to the amusement of an elderly lady who volunteered that she hadn't touched her toes for thirty years.

As I languished in the luxury of the wine coloured sofa, so thoughtfully provided, I became conscious of the picture in front of me. I complimented myself that since my retirement, I had taken more interest in my wife's ability to paint and had begun to enjoy "Water Colour Challenge" on television. I detected her ability to interpret shadows and even on our walks, she would point out that on a sunny day the underside of clouds are darker than the tops, but the reverse is true at sunset. I was applying my knowledge to this picture, consisting of a mother and three children sitting or standing around a garden bench. The mother's face had captured my attention. The softness of her cheeks and her obvious devotion to her girls was all too apparent.

"That's called 'Le Banc de Jardin', painted by James Tissot."

Suddenly, I was aware that my hand was covered by the warm fingers of a smart fashionable middle aged lady who must have been resident when I arrived. Not wanting to make an issue of our proximity, I smiled, encouraging her to continue.

"Yes, Tissot was French and came to London in 1871 to enjoy the Thames lifestyle. His model, Kathleen Newton, an Irish divorcee, lived with him until she died of tuberculosis in 1882, leading to his return to France. His counterpart at that time was John Grimshaw. Neither of the two were insiders of the London art set but Andrew Lloyd Webber, whose collection this is, has always insisted that he collects pictures, not artists and these are two of his favourites for combining Domestic and Operatic."

"Not many people know that!" I laughed.

"Grimshaw's best are over there, 'Wimbledon Park' and 'Chyll Beck'. Look at those trees." I was relieved at the release of my hand as she waved at a picture behind us.

"I don't pretend to know anything about art," I ventured, but then regretted it because, on reflection, my words could have been construed as inferring that she may be exaggerating. "What I mean, is, I know nothing. Well, not quite nothing, because I noticed in the next room that the real name of the famous painter, Canoletti, was Giovani Canal."

"Even fewer people know that," she quipped, gripping my hand with both of hers and we both laughed at her quick wit. "I'm Bernice, call me Bernie, what's yours?"

It then hit me. Her face was identical to the mother in the picture. Soft looking, slightly peach coloured, intent and beautifully manicured. A sideways glance at the painting confirmed that even her hair had a similar quiff. I was experiencing a strange, mental situation to which I was unaccustomed. This lady was calling the tune and I was unable to change the wavelength.

"Arthur, but I nearly said, a large brandy."

"A large brandy it will be, but after lunch and that will be my treat. Before we leave here, though, I don't want you to miss the two outstanding pieces in the exhibition. Come."

I knew it. I was hooked like the proverbial trout. One minute I was doing my own thing, just like on any of the previous three hundred and sixty five days and now, suddenly, bang! I was caught in an artistic whirlwind, being whisked away, out of control. Why on earth had I chosen to come here? My wife had waxed lyrical about the display a couple of months ago and having had cause to visit the New Zealand Tourist Board earlier this morning to finalise a holiday, the Academy was a convenient building in which I could shelter from the rain for a couple of hours. My wife was away visiting our daughter for two days and my holiday plans were destined to be a surprise present on her return. But the tables were being turned and it was me on the surprise train.

Her arm was through mine as we walked determinedly into the next room. There in the centre was a white marble nude. It was exactly as my wife had described the exhibit.

"Well, what do you think of that?" Bernice mused and before she had a chance to drift into the realms of fantasy or fact, I interrupted.

"Ah yes, Antonio Fritto's white marble 'Nude Reclining in a Hammock', beautifully lifelike isn't she?"

"Marvellous, you've been teasing me haven't you? And who have you seen in a hammock, I wonder." Silence. "Let's try this one."

I remained silent while Bernice gave chapter and verse about Fred Leighton's 'Standing Nude' and Sir Edward Pointer's 'The Cave of Storm Nymphs', a conglomeration of cavorting nakedness. She appeared to have an obsession with bodies but I consoled myself by knowing that she couldn't possibly be after mine!

"What was your favourite picture," she asked as we climbed into a taxi.

"Actually, I know little about the exhibits except for what I read in the brochure. I was only kidding when I pretended to know the marble thing. The one that took my attention was Marcus Stone's 'The Railway Station'. There are so many people in the picture, but the interesting point was that it showed the first police arrest having used the telephone, or telegraph as they called it."

Our hands remained entwined throughout the short journey except when she leant over to plant a gentle kiss on my cheek. "That's for giving me a laugh today. Now let's see what you think of Simpson's".

Without giving away the fact that this Strand gentlemen's restaurant had been a regular haunt of mine for many years before my retirement, I allowed my escort to plan and order the entire feast and except for the traditional sovereign for the white-aproned beef waiter, Bernice hosted in an elegant fashion, relaxing only to allow me to stand the second round of Napoleon.

Bernice was a conversationalist. She did all, or most of the talking, allowing me to interject occasionally with one of my funnies. When I mentioned that I liked her discussion technique, I added that a woman has the last word in any argument and anything that a man says after that is the beginning of a new argument. This set her giggling so I tried her with a philosophy about Happiness. To be happy with a man, you must understand him a lot and love him a little. To be happy with a woman, you must love her a lot and never try to understand her at all.

Bernice rocked with laughter but that was my undoing. "Right, it's back to my place for coffee and then I'm off on my travels. Again, no arguing." My god, what was I letting myself into? I was arm-locked into a taxi and in less than a quarter of a mile we were at 'her place', the Waldorf Hotel. Oh no! I stayed here for five months in 1978. On one occasion, after a heavy night in Le Bistingo restaurant, I had returned rather the worse for wear and on meeting the reception staff the following morning, the lady said, 'You enjoyed your evening sir? When you returned, you stood over there at the double doors leading to the lounge and I had to come and tell you that that particular lift was not working. I'm not saying who put you to bed!'

I was close to a dilemma. I felt good but I am not flippant with my affections. Supposing she really wanted sex. Why else would she be so demanding and complimentary? Perhaps, if she really is going on her travels, she won't want to get too involved. I was still convincing myself in the lift that she was harmless, when one hand went north around my neck and the other one went south. The kiss was wet and daring and I was saved by the sudden jerk as we stopped at the fifth and a scruffy haired 'oldest-swinger-in-town guy' joined us.

"Hi Bernard," he said to my startled companion, "glad to see yer. Got this video, a real corker. Your room or mine? Wait a minute. Don't tell me you're going for some fresh? He doesn't look like one of us."

Taking my chance, I dashed between the two of them and leapt through an adjoining door and raced down the stairs two at a time, not daring to look back or think of anything but the safety of the Reception area. But there was no refuge there. As I arrived exhausted and leg weary, the lift door parted and amidst the group alighting was my guide, looking anything but the attractive companion of an hour ago. Her smooth complexion was now showing the frowns of the true male Bernard. In the haven of the good old London cab, I calmed.

"Had a memorable lunch, guv?"

As I remonstrated with myself for being so naïve, I replied, "Just a chance acquaintance."

LOVE AND MARRIAGE

"Write a story of not more than 50 words, using a Proverb as the basis."

I chose the old Arab Proverb depicting the Difference between Love and Marriage. "Love is when a man gazes into the starry sky as he walks through life. Marriage is the hole that he falls into."

"My heart melted under her captivating beauty. Her smile, sparkling eyes and sensual voice reflected an affectionate adoration. Soft passionate fingers beckoned me into her life. I would gaze at the starry stars as I walked through life. Marriage, rewarding my initial infatuation, was my doom."

LOVE AND THE STARS

Whilst we are talking about Stars, you will discover that I don't go along with the media contentions that the stars can influence your destiny. But I enjoyed researching some aspects of magazine zodiac birth signs predictions in order to write the following story.

Perhaps there is some semblance of truth in it after all ……..

LOVE AND THE STARS

LOVE IS ……. LOVE IS …… Love is difficult to define. It is a personal thing. It is a feeling known only to each one of us and probably, it is different for everyone. All we can say, is that we "know" when Love has struck. The hurt, the pain, the distrust, perhaps jealousy, adoration, extreme happiness, the sudden upsurge of enough strength to move mountains, the desire to please, the desire to squeeze the living daylights out of our loved-one, all combine to tell the world that we are in love.

It's easier to explain what Love is NOT. Contrary to popular belief amongst the younger generation, Love is not the Quickie behind the bicycle shed at school. Neither is it the result of being labelled "great in bed" by the Third Year at University. Even "Marriage" is not a true symbol of Love. No, Love is personal.

The Arabs have a proverb defining the difference between Love and Marriage. It states that Love is when a man gazes at the stars in the sky as he walks through life. Marriage is the hole that he falls into.

The notion that the stars influence our love life is also bunkum. All that clap-trap available every day in the press and heartthrob magazines amazes me that people can be so gullible as to be taken in by the apparent sincerity of the forecasts. I mean to say … how can a statement, "Love will entice you to go far today; prepare yourself for breaking those chains that are responsible for your dull routines", apply to a much travelled business man and a poor old bed-ridden paralysed person just because they were both born on January 3rd? Well, that's what I used to say until a rather bizarre weekend a couple of years ago in our early thirties.

My references to what Love is NOT, are relevant to this story because I first met Gerry at school where we began a lasting friendship, staying together through university and even starting similar careers with an international distributor. He was a bike shed specialist, winning his spurs with a married woman at the age of twelve and learnt the art of getting his Prep work for lectures at university prepared for him by the girls who he was servicing.

Following our graduation, his conquests continued unabated through the Accounts and Commercial Departments at work, so the firm was not only paying him a handsome salary, but they provided him with the fodder for his insatiable appetite. In other words, he was God's answer to women, or so he thought. But the net was closing in and Beryl had been struck by Eros's arrow, as well as Gerry's.

"Why don't you settle down and get married?" I conjectured with him over a drink, discussing his problem.

"You don't buy a book when you can join a library," he retorted.

His solution was simple. He opened talks with his employer to secure himself a lucrative post in the merchant navy side of the organisation. This enabled him to succumb to Beryl's demands to become engaged, thus protecting his library ticket on his return to the UK between foreign travels. His freedom, whilst abroad, attracted another dimension, that of tasting the fruits of the Caribbean and the more basic feasts of the hardened Malay daughters.

It came as a surprise to me, not without a measure of disbelief, when Gerry asked me to be his best man at his wedding to be held on Saturday, 21st August, just five weeks away. He would be in the Mediterranean until the 14th but he would leave me to liaise with Beryl over the practicalities of the wedding, including the honeymoon booking. Love was about to blossom.

Naturally, my desire to ensure that the big day would have no hiccoughs meant that I had need to contact Beryl almost daily, checking on the church layout, the car details and of course, the honeymoon. I was beginning to feel sorry for her as I covered up over doubts regarding his sincerity. His only phone call to her during the final week was to tell her that his return had been delayed until Thursday, 19th and asking me to organise his stag night.

It was whilst I was in his flat awaiting his arrival, that I glanced at the Horoscope in the magazine that I had picked up. "What rubbish," I thought, glancing nonchalantly at Leo, that covered both Gerry and me. "Venus spreads love and light throughout your life. The 21st will be the best day for forging new romantic alliances.

Work tirelessly to smooth the passage of Love. Consider the heart desire of family elders. Brush up on your responsibilities and oil the memory box. Above all, don't waste an opportunity."

"OK, so Gerry is getting married," I thought, "but I hope that it doesn't mean that he is going to prang Beryl's granny. God forbid."

But I was wasting my time hanging around for him. At 9pm the phone rang.

"Hi. I'm sorry mate but I won't be there until tomorrow evening. I've got this problem in Southampton and need to smooth over a little domestic misunderstanding. Tell you about it. Cheers." And he was gone. So I left the flat, went home and prepared my stuff for the wedding and returned Friday afternoon, ready to blast the rogue for putting me in this spot. What was that the Horoscope said? Brush up on your responsibilities. Yes, so I phoned Beryl to check that everything was in place, only to be told that Gerry had rung to tell her that he was at home and he would see her at the church. "Keep him sober for tomorrow", was Beryl's last words to me as she downed the phone.

The restless Friday night came and went, with no sign of the groom. To pass the time, I rehearsed my speech about the attributes of the lovely bridesmaid, thanking the groom on her behalf for the present, which I had bought and wrapped. As Saturday morning dawned, I changed the speech, injecting a "funny" that a card had just arrived from the groom saying that he would meet Beryl at the honeymoon hotel.

At 10am an inebriated Gerry burst through the door, tripped over the rug, sprawled across the floor and with his case crashing open with the impact, he begged me to pay the taxi driver. The ensuing panic matched anything that the Keystone Cops could have invented. It was only when I manhandled him into the shower that I made him realise that he had two hours to get to the church, that is, if he had any intentions of going.

"Of course I am," he spluttered, "I wouldn't miss a wedding, especially my own. I enjoyed the first two and three is my lucky number." He was in the process of confiding in me that he had already had two, or was it three ceremonies abroad when the phone rang. It was Beryl's father. Beryl was distraught with worry and needed some reassurance, which I was able to give, out of earshot of the noisy shower area. By now, I was caught up in the subterfuge with no escape. In two hours I would be adding perjury to my sins when the vicar would ask for "Any just cause why this couple should not …"

Gerry lay in the well of the shower when I returned and it was now a case of sharp tactics and brute force to save the day. I turned on the cold water and stood clear. It worked. An agonised Gerry scrambled from the shower leaving a trail of water cascading into the bathroom. In a moment of sheer desperation, I grabbed his deflated sign of manhood and threatened to pull it off if he didn't bring himself round and make some headway. Beryl didn't deserve him but I was going to do my utmost to drag him to the church, with or without his co-operation. Our eyes met and we fell about laughing at the thought of what an onlooker would have seen.

Things started to take shape but time was not on our side. Gerry's new shirt bought in Hong Kong was not the size depicted on the label. The tie would need to have a loose knot; fashionable, we laughed. Likewise, the suit, made at the same tailor, had been made for the Hunchback of Notre Dame but didn't look too bad if the jacket remained unbuttoned. There was no time to clean his shoes so we agreed to swap footwear, thinking that nobody would notice if my shoes were dirty.

We should have left at least twenty minutes earlier, but in a crisis, it calls for desperate measures and luck. A phone call to Beryl's house gave us the boost that we required. She also would be late, because her dad answered the phone as I replaced the receiver. With a free run of traffic, the best that we could hope for, would be to arrive fifteen minutes late which might be enough to beat Beryl. It was only after we had set off that Gerry reminded me that he had left his going away case at the flat and this turned my stomach over as I realised also that the Honeymoon tickets were also in my other coat.

"What sort of best man are you?" he laughed. "I'm not having you organise my funeral". We were still chuckling when I caught sight of the white car ahead. It was the company providing the bride's family transport and as we passed, there was Beryl, shocked at the sight of seeing us. Shaking her fist, she was not happy and obviously had asked the driver to slow down.

But fate was about to cast its worst spell over us. As we parked the car by the church gate, we could see that the guests were all inside, with the one bridesmaid standing in the entrance. On entering the churchyard we saw a solitary old lady pacing across the path. Seeing us and recognising Gerry, she immediately rushed at him, waving her umbrella and reprimanded him for causing so much anxiety. To our complete horror, she uttered a faint scream and fell to the ground. If panic was the word to describe our earlier actions, it was now time for extreme panic.

The lady was Beryl's Granny and had a known heart condition. In the seconds that followed, Gerry had made the shocking discovery that her pulse had stopped. She was dead.

"We can't let Beryl see her. Her day is already upset. What can we do?"

"Quick," I replied, "let's move her to the rear of the church. You take her legs."

It was inconceivable that we should have done this terrible deed, but it was a case of "any port in a storm", as Gerry described it. We had just enough time to dial 999 on the mobile and call for an ambulance, explaining where granny could be found, before the white car turned the corner. As we raced into the church, barely speaking to the bridesmaid, I told Gerry that I would leave the church when we heard the ambulance and would sort out the details. Luckily nobody saw the episode and we gained our places in the front pew we managed to avoid the gaze of the well-wishers and tried to regain our breath.

"You've got a nerve, Gerry, playing our Beryl along like this". Her mother had crossed the isle and with her lip quivering, she added in a loud voice, "she'd be well rid of you and all your philandering. Don't think that we can't see through you" and with tears welling, she returned to her seat, head bowed.

"I don't think I can go through with this," whispered Gerry.

"Well, you'll have to, the reception has cost a bomb and has been paid for. In any case, it's too late, she's here." And the organ announced the arrival of Beryl in the entrance.

I grabbed his arm and pushed him into the isle, sensing that I was the only person trying to fulfil the object of the day. A very cross Beryl joined us and just as I thought we would be under way, the vicar moved close to me and stuttered, "I haven't been paid yet."

"Is that unusual?" asked Gerry, who then nudged me to do he honours. Having established the amount, I slipped the notes to the vicar, who, without offering me any change, proceeded with "Dearly Beloved, ..."

He welcomed us all and was about to get into his stride and ask the vulnerable question whether anybody knew of reasons why the ceremony should not take place, when the wail of the ambulance drowned his words and Gerry ran from the church, closely followed by me. To my horror, instead of going to the ambulance, Gerry vaulted over the low wall of the churchyard and headed for the main road.

In desperation, I hastily directed the paramedics to the rear of the church and hurried back into the scene of distress and bewilderment. Seizing on the coward's way out, I revealed that, on our arrival at the churchyard, Gerry had seen granny resting, obviously ill. She had waved us away and as we hurried to the church, Gerry had phoned for a doctor, I thought. I expanded the story sufficiently to give the paramedics ample time to diagnose the inevitable. Beryl's mother had been too distressed to notice that her mother was even missing and in an attempt to redress the situation, led a posse including me, outside.

Luck had decided to smile on me and we were just able to witness the final act of the stretcher being pushed inside the ambulance, the slamming of the door and the immediate departure. Everybody assumed that Gerry had accompanied granny to the hospital and this released me from the conjecture of his whereabouts. Nobody seemed to be taking control of the fiasco until the vicar joined us and announced that, although it was obvious that the wedding had been postponed, he would be unable to refund his fee.

"And would you all mind removing the cars from the vicinity, because the next wedding is due to take place in fifteen minutes."

I sidled up to Beryl, put my arms around her and suggested that, as the reception had been financed, why not go to the hotel and await the report from Gerry at the hospital. With no other sensible solution, Beryl's father advised the remainder of the congregation that the "Do" was off, but the reception would continue. He diplomatically said that he would divulge more, after he had downed a brandy or two.

So, a day that had begun with trepidation, gradually developed under the spell of Leo, smoothing the passage of Love, mindful of a pending heart attack and, finally, after getting well-oiled, I prevented an opportunity from escaping. Yes, there were tears, threats and many "I told you so's". The honeymoon had also been financed and a static caravan can be quite romantic. Oh, and another thing. Love blossomed and Beryl and I are expecting our second boy, Leo in a month's time.

THE PEAR TREE

My father survived the trench warfare of the First World War and although he said little of the terror and diabolical conditions under which the soldiers fought, he mentioned the trauma of being court-martialled for losing one of the first mobile machine guns in the mud.

Although this story is not about him, I had him in mind when I tried to imagine the mental stress that soldiers and their loved ones experienced.

THE PEAR TREE

"It is the decision of this Court Martial that the two defendants Lance Corporal Charles Cochran and Private Ben White have been found guilty of the loss, by negligence, of one mobile machine gun, its carriage and associated ammunition, property of His Majesty's Government."

There was a gasp in the make-shift courtroom. Private White released an uncontrolled "No!", before being restrained by his defending Officer. The Lance Corporal retained his immaculate upright stance.

"The Court will reconvene at 1000 hrs tomorrow, when I shall pass sentence."

"May I respectfully remind the President that there can be only one sentence for …"

"Thank you Gerald, I wish to speak with you and the defending Captain in my room."

The officers dispersed. The guard and escort screamed orders at the guilty prisoners and led them away to the guard room for what may prove to be their last night on this earth.

Adelaide sat alone in her mother's garden using the great magnolia tree's shadow to shield her from the Spring sunshine. The postman had passed her gate again. Still no news from Ben. A single tear hesitated beneath her eyelid before making a curved line across her colourless cheek and falling to her blouse. She had lost the ability to cry. Although she posted a letter to a far-off address in France every Friday, she knew in her heart that few, if any, would ever be read by him. The last letter received from Ben had been written three months earlier. He had sounded bright, though freezing cold, but she detected a hint that he had been more fortunate than his village mates who were posted to the front line, whereas he was enjoying comparative calm as a supply orderly in a chateau miles behind the lines.

This feeling of security gave her comfort, and hope. Hope that one day they could re-live those magical moments just after his seventeenth birthday when he proudly announced that he had received his call-up papers. For the umpteenth time she fantasised over the afternoon when he had overcome his shyness and taken her to the orchard to disclose his plans for the army call-up. It was there that he had expressed his undying love for her. He would fight honourably for the King but would return to marry her if she would accept his proposal. Adelaide had done so willingly, at which Ben had cried with disbelief and then, as if to seal their betrothal, he pleaded with her to let him caress her under her chemise.

During an afternoon of bliss he had carved their initials on a pear tree. They were desperately in love in a way that convinced them that separation would not change them. Their early letters compounded their feelings, both relying on the knowledge that the continued expressions of love would give strength to the other. Adelaide learnt from the newspaper reports that Ben must be suffering extreme hardships and now, with the letters becoming more infrequent, she felt so helpless. Ben had been away two years and Adelaide began to see her life slipping away.

"Those bloody bloodthirsty bastards. Especially that pansy, Gerald, Bastard." Ben was sobbing.

"Don't give up, Blanco. I've got a notion in me piss that we may not get the chop tomorrow. That President must have had some reason for not sending us straight to the squad."

The door of the guardroom opened and the defence Captain entered, smiling. He had been a strength to the two men in the hearing. It was he who had described the insurmountable depth of mud which had prevented the truck from reaching the Front Line to deliver the new machine gun to the Section of the battalion trying to establish a foothold on the eastern trenches of the Arras offensive. Three weeks earlier thousands of men and their weapons had been transported through the maze of underground tunnels from the Town Hall in the centre of Arras to the forward trenches two miles away, without the Germans knowing. But now the surprise element had worn thin and an urgent call had been sent to the Supply Division to get this special gun, one of the first of its kind, to sweep the area.

Blanco and Charlie had made good progress with the truck until they hit the mud zone. Torrential rain had made the road impassable. The sergeant driver ordered the two men to unload the gun and push it to the destination. After two hours they had travelled half a mile and were beginning to reach the rearguard trenches. They saw the plight of the men trying to move within the parameters of the lines, but pushing the obstinate trolley was almost impossible.

An hour later they found themselves approaching a copse. It was here that they made the fateful mistake of trying to bypass it. Their map indicated that a track would shorten the route by about a mile. At first the downhill terrain was in their favour, but as it levelled out, the ground was like quicksand. Charlie sank up to his knees in wet mud and was screaming for help. Ben clung on to the gun that was sinking fast. At that moment a small platoon in the area arrived, having heard the cries. Both men were saved but first the wheels, then the gun sank out of sight into the morass.

"Cheer up lads," came the captain, "I think you may get a warning and a posting, although it may be the Front."

It was the Front.

They were the furthest forward trenches of the Arras lines; the area where the gun should have been delivered. It was Ben's first experience of trench warfare. The water was ankle deep and the mud underneath made movement treacherous. The smell of urine and excreta filled the nostrils. Within minutes of arriving, Charlie failed to keep his head down and a bullet hit his helmet, but he survived. All the men looked tired and mud-splattered. Some seemed to be asleep on their feet. Others stood, leaning against the trench wall, smoking. Others just stood, trying to keep their rifle dry.

Suddenly all hell let loose. Allied guns were firing from behind, towards the Germans. The shells whined as they sped on their way. And then came the awful whistles. The men all came alive and alert, however tired. Each time the sarge gave two blasts, six men would mount the three ladders up the sides of the trench and disappear into no-mans land. Men prayed as their turn came. Two froze to the spot, out of sheer fear. The sergeant didn't believe in fear and when one of the men refused to go, he was shot and an orderly quickly removed the body. Ben was sick. Then it was his turn. As he climbed the steps, he thought momentarily of Adelaide.

"I'm coming home," he shouted and rushed blindly in the direction of his predecessors.

He awoke in the Field Hospital. He felt nothing. He remembered nothing. His head was bandaged and a rough sling held his arm to his body. A nurse saw that he was awake.

"Try and sleep soldier. It will be better for you."

He needed no telling. Sleep came naturally with the morphine. He slept long. Nightmares made him cry out for mercy but none came. Then the pain took over and his cries brought the nurse and surgeon to his bedside.

"More morphine. We must get him out of here. See to it, nurse."

The nurse, though hardened by the sight of the poor wretches passing through the post, squeezed his hand and smiled. Something triggered a special demand in her mind and she knelt close to Ben.

"Hold on, soldier, you and me are going to make it." Even she didn't believe it.

Adelaide finally made the decision to volunteer for nursing duties at the Cottage Hospital. Posters around the town said that the country had a duty to care for our brave men. She had heard the news that the Armistice had been signed and the war was over. Her sadness over Ben had slowly subsided. Not having heard from him for over a year, she had accepted that he was dead. She was growing used to the company of Bernard, a doctor in the next village, many years her senior. So nursing gave her a common interest and became a therapy for passing time. The deep love that had been born in her in the orchard had never blossomed into adulthood. She would never be able to kindle that spirit. She knew no other life.

Nurse Elsie supervised the movement of soldier No 36548762 to the Long Term Wing of the Amiens hospital where she was determined to enhance his quality of life. An unexpected turn of events happened when it transpired that the boisterous soldier in the next bed was Charlie. On hearing the attempts of the nurse to discover the personal details of Ben, he suggested that she asked him about Adelaide who lived near his home in Dorset. During the ensuing three weeks his memory was prompted but he began to be reluctant to talk for fear of Adelaide discovering the extent of his injuries. At the same time Elsie spent long periods holding Ben's hand and generally giving him an urge to live.

Behind the bandages shielding his missing eye, Elsie was certain that a smile occasionally appeared. He was beginning to have an effect on her. The cross fertilisation of minds was having results. The desire to live was compulsive. Ben hated the moments when Elsie had to turn to other pressing duties.

Adelaide's world suddenly turned upside down. Ben's sister ran to her with the news that Ben was alive in France and that his mother thought that she should go and see him. For two nights Adelaide did not sleep, unable to draw up the courage to go. She was not sure that her feelings were strong enough. Eventually her friend Bernard persuaded her that she had a duty. As the journey unfolded, her fear turned to expectancy and then to love for Ben. She quickened her steps through the hospital grounds to the Long Term Ward. But she was unprepared for the shock that faced her. As she opened his door Adelaide gulped and let out a gasp. The man in the chair by the bed was in an embrace with a nurse.

Overcoming her bewilderment, she moved towards the bed, extending her hand towards Ben. To her horror, there was no arm to take hers. Elsie suggested that she and Adelaide should leave the room and talk outside, which gave Adelaide time to clear her mind. She learned that Ben had no legs, only one arm and would probably lose his sight. Sickened by the news, Adelaide rushed back to the bedside and rained kisses on his cheeks.

"I love you Ben darling. I always will. I will care for you. Come home".

Ben remained silent, in a state of shock and unable to come to terms with the situation. He doubted in his own mind whether or not he would even survive another operation that was imminent. He withdrew from Adelaide.

"No. It's over. I have no love for you, or life. You shouldn't have come"

Adelaide rushed from the hospital, disillusioned and grieved. She wandered aimlessly along war-torn streets. Alone and unwanted, she rued her decision to seek her lover. The re-awakened yearning for the return of Ben to her life had been crudely rejected, firstly by seeing the embrace and then the indifference of Ben. With darkness approaching and heavy rain drenching her clothes and straggling her hair, Adelaide tripped and fell into a muddy path. Uncontrollable sobbing took over and she lay shaking with utter despair. Her life was in ruins and she now shared Ben's desire to die.

The biting cold injected a need for her to move but on getting up, her legs were reluctant. Without wanting to control her emotions she staggered a hundred yards, before falling again, this time into the path of an army truck. She died instantly.

As Adelaide was running from the ward Ben had gone into a coma from which he never recovered. Elsie tried repeatedly to encourage him to rally, but without success. He died without being aware that his nurse also wanted him to join her for life.

Another white wooden cross joined the thousands of remembrance crosses in the local war cemetery, near Arras, "Private Ben "Blanco" White. Died February 1919", whilst hundreds of miles away in Dorset, a simple plaque appeared in a pear orchard, "Our Darling Adelaide died of a broken heart, February, 1919"

THE MEASURE OF LOVE

I believe that we all have the ability to express our feelings in verse, and I have to admit being surprised many years ago when I produced the following poem. I was away from home, lying in a lonely hotel room bemoaning my lot and I wanted to tell my wife what she really meant to me.

The opening couple of lines set me on course and I still enjoy confirming that the sentiments are as strong today, as ever.

THE MEASURE OF LOVE

Have you ever gazed into the dark deep sea
Fearing the wonders of its power and might?
Have you stood and marvelled at the vast night sky
At a frosty time when the stars shine bright?

Have you roamed on the moors through heather and fern
Seeing nothing but moors till the horizon is met?
Seen hurricanes work, carving paths in their wake
Eating at trees, homes and anything, sucked into their net?

Have you thought of inventions since earth first began
Gasping at space and the miles to the sun
Have you watched at a birth when a babe first appears,
And the joy of producing a girl or a son.

Have you planted your seeds at the start of a year
Giving joy and relief at the sign of a shoot?
Have you watched with mixed feelings at seeing the snow
How can plants live to bear flowers and fruit?

These feelings of depth and wonderful joy
Can't ever approach, whatever I do,
The burning desire locked inside my head
Measuring my undying Love for you.

THE SECRET ROOM

I was wading through a photograph album looking for inspiration to meet the demands of my writing group's project, using the above title. Pictures of Le Puy in Central France held the key.

A writer's best results are usually obtained when the work is an account of circumstances actually experienced, rather than researched subjects. The album jerked my memory to the days when we turned a corner whilst travelling north through France and were confronted with the amazing sight of a huge red Madonna perched on a volcanic pinnacle. A plaque indicated that it was a monument to remember the French resistance fighters during the German occupation in the 2nd world war.

THE SECRET ROOM

The next time that you find yourself in the Massif Central region of France, make sure that you visit Le Puy. You will not be disappointed. The attraction of the city is its setting. Three volcanic rocks tower above the place and the most spindly of them, the chimney of the old volcano, is crowned by a small Romanesque chapel. On a nearby peak, lording above the whole area is a magnificent huge red Madonna reached after a tiring staircase climb. A plaque at the foot dedicates the monument to the memory of the French Resistance who plagued the invaders during the Second World War occupation by the Germans. Reading the plaque always puts a lump in my throat as I recall a three month period in 1941 when I lived with those brave people.

I mentioned the chapel because I befriended Pierre, the son of the Pastor whilst on a youth exchange visit prior to the war. During my short stay we made an amazing discovery in the chapel graveyard situated at the foot of the volcanic spindle. Amongst the numerous family vaults, we stumbled across an ornate structure whose metal railings were broken even though the gate was padlocked, as was the wooden entrance. Being inquisitive, Pierre soon found that, by lifting the side stanchion, a section of the vault entrance opened, allowing us access to the steps into the chamber.

Later that day and armed with torches, we returned, descended the steps with great fear and trepidation and gaped at two coffins, side by side. Although dusty, a plate gave the same date of burial for both of the deceased, February, 1890. Neither of us admitted being scared and we planned to use the place as a den for the remainder of the holiday without telling anybody. In fact, we took an oil lamp to give us better lighting and drew sketches using the coffins as tables.

Had it not been for a chance remark that I made during an Officers' Mess Dinner at RAF Manston, the story would have ended there. But my comment about knowing the Le Puy area as a boy, led to the coincidence of me being infiltrated into the Resistance network just outside the city to help coordinate the escape of British airmen. The secret tomb was an ideal safe-house where each man could lay low for a couple of days awaiting the call to be escorted to join a small boat that sailed regularly along the Loire.

The location of the hideaway did not have the support of all the Resistance team, some reacting on moral grounds, saying that it was desecrating the memory of the dead. But the alternative of putting local folk at risk by being found harbouring escaped airmen soon won them over and the vault was made more welcoming. The old oil lamp was replaced by a larger one and covers were brought to hide the rightful inhabitants. The door was adjusted to ensure that we couldn't be locked in accidentally and chairs and sacks of clothing appeared. We achieved the objective of disguising the true scary atmosphere of being entombed. It was after the first successful use of the hideout that I made a welcome discovery. Noticing that several stones behind the coffins were loose, I managed to remove four, revealing an adjacent vault. We had an instant annexe. Fortunately it was empty, though smaller. All that was necessary was to force the lock on the outside to give us a much-needed alternative escape route. The removal of two further stones made access to both vaults easier and spare stones from the cemetery enabled us to block the gap from either side in an emergency.

My main task was to operate the radio and the second vault was an ideal place to house it. My initial call to London when I had set up the station proved successful and my fears of loss of reception and transmission did not materialise. The powerful set worked well and was the envy of the French. My first line of contact with the Resistance was the baker Jacques and this worked well because he ensured that our vault was kept stocked with food, not only for me but also any passing trade. He lived and worked two hundred yards from the cemetery fence, next door to the undertaker, Jean, with whom I lodged.

It was Jean's hearse that was used to transport our first airman to the river, but the audacity of such a trick could be used only occasionally and we had other plans for each time. Many Germans were stationed in the area and were well aware of the Resistance ploys, but while there was a lull in serious acts of sabotage, normal life continued with few soldiers on the streets, especially at night. A second and then a third airman passed through our hands without any sign of default. The Secret Tomb was playing its part.

Then things started heating up. A plane crashed locally in daylight and the pilot was seen by everybody as he parachuted down. On landing, he was whisked away by the French and this annoyed the Germans. Threats of reprisals were accompanied by a curfew and suddenly we felt exposed. Jacques' bakery was raided and searched but although they found nothing, it was clear that he was on a suspects list. My point of contact was, therefore, changed and I spent more time away from Jean's, fearing that he also may be under suspicion. I then got some alarming news from London.

"Three leading resistance workers in Lyon have been arrested by the Germans, thus virtually annihilating the network in the city. I will say this only once. There is obviously an informer in your area."

Having confided with Jean and Jacques I waited for their reaction, which was immediate. They had news about the airman and were hoping to get him out of their patch. He was injured and needed treatment, but this had been arranged, making him comfortable enough to get on the trail in a week's time. Meanwhile, Jacques would put out a false plan into the network, just to see whether there was any unusual activity amongst the Germans. Hopefully, if there was no leak, this would clear the way for the real evacuation.

We removed everything out of the vault and set up a watch rota in the cemetery during the day of the hoax action. The deadline for the arrival had been set for 1900 hrs, just before dusk. All day we waited in pairs, tending flowers at the headstones, sweeping paths and watering plants. By 1800hrs our nerves were on edge, fearing that the wrath of the Germans was about to unleash itself. At 1830 Jean, bedecked in his best black suit and hat, walked quickly through the cemetery gates towards the tiny service chapel and passing within feet of two of us hiding behind bushes.

"There is a car at the gate with two occupants, a German and a French civilian. Do nothing. Don't move."

Jean walked to a newly dug grave, checked the tarpaulin covering it and walked smartly back to the gate. Immediately after he had gone, two men emerged, heading in the direction of our vault. One was removing a revolver from his belt and the second walked nervously by his side. Having pointed to the vault the civilian turned and moved away in our direction.

My heart sank. Tears came uncontrollably to my eyes. I didn't want to believe it.

Pierre, my schoolboy friend, was a French Traitor.

ST. VALENTINE'S DAY

"Write an amusing short story about St. Valentine's day". OK, we all know it is about love, but how could I make it amusing? I was not in a serious frame of mind, which was fortunate, because we were not given much time to produce our offering.

So why re-invent the wheel. I'll introduce a series of old jokes as I go along! The chairman asked for a Short story, so that is what it will be …… short.

ST. VALENTINE'S DAY

Everybody has an annual special day for celebrating. Perhaps it's their wedding anniversary, or even the day they got divorced. It's that special something that turns the tummy over when that day dawns each year. Sport fanatics celebrate the day when England won the World cup in 1966 or the Ashes in 1953. Religion lends itself to special days, hence Christmas Day or the last day of Ramadan. It doesn't have to be a happy event. Les Dawson always maintained that he couldn't predict when his special days would occur. He waited until he saw the mice throwing themselves onto the traps, thus announcing the arrival of his mother-in-law and he knew straight away that it was time to go to the pub.

February 14th is my special day. To start with, I was born on that day. Dad was not too happy. He wanted a girl. When I come to think of it, my mother wasn't overjoyed either. She maintained that the plastic bag over my head was an attempt to keep me fresh. At school, we were encouraged to keep a diary and after a few years I noticed that on three consecutive February 14ths, I was caned by the headmaster. The first time was for telling a joke in class to my mate during an English lesson when the teacher was talking about stories with a moral. The teacher made me stand and repeat the story to the whole class. It was about my grandfather in the Great War. He was in the trenches during a battle and all he had left was a bottle of whiskey, five rounds of ammunition and his bayonet. All of his colleagues had been killed. So he fired his five rounds killing five Germans. He then drank the whiskey, fixed the bayonet and charged the German trenches, killing all fifteen of those remaining.

"So, what's the moral of that story," asked the teacher.

"You don't muck about with Granddad when he's pissed."

The second time featured Granddad again. I was late back to school after lunch and when asked by the teacher why I was late, I said that Granddad had got burned. So after getting the cane the teacher asked if it was a bad burn, to which I replied, "They don't muck about at the Crematorium."

The third year was more embarrassing and involved Phyllis, a girl with a pigtail to whom I had sent a love letter during a lesson on Valentine Day and its meaning. Unfortunately, we were caught after school in the Art Room. I'm sure that the Art Master was up to no good with Miss Pringle when they caught us.

I began my first job as a Tax Clerk in the Inland Revenue on February 14th and was rewarded by a thief who stole my new bike from outside the St. Martins Le Grand office in London. He even had the audacity to remove the railings to which the bike was chained. The following year I joined the RAF for my National Service. Yes, the date was February 14th. Certainly, this was not a happy day and my induction was not helped when I was telling Irish jokes in the NAAFI, only to find that the Corporal in charge was Irish. I tried to explain that he was not the Paddy in my story, who thought he ought to be in the Guinness Book of Records for doing a 25 piece jigsaw puzzle in three days when on the box it said for 2/3 years. I soon found out that my living quarters named Valentine Block had a patio area and as I obviously liked puzzles, the Corporal gave me the task of taking up the stones and relaying them, as a punishment over the next three evenings.

On my return to civilian life two years later, on February 14th , Valentine Day had become a focal point of more important events in my life, affairs of the heart. Needless to say, Valentine Day cards were in abundance but I had already learnt that it is a dangerous pastime assuming that so-and-so must have sent that saucy card. If that person had wanted to get involved, surely she wouldn't have waited until that day to air her desires. This philosophy prevented me from wasting money

THE LUCK OF GEORGE

A national newspaper carried the following throw-away story: "Man in car found at the bottom of a cliff. Foul play is not suspected." Surely there must be a strange background to this item. I wracked my brains to find a likely solution.

Sometimes I base my stories on characters that I know and I can picture their reactions as the final chapter emerges. Perhaps a writer even predicts a possible end to that pompous individual.

THE LUCK OF GEORGE

GEORGE AND JUDY
George maintained that people made their own luck in this world and he would live to be a hundred and five. It was alright for him. He enjoyed the best of health. His wife, Judy who also shared his philosophy, supported him in his main hobbies. Both were active, playing at the same golf club with respectable handicaps and enjoying the social side of the club, of which he was Social Secretary. A weekly six mile walk together was commonplace. He also enjoyed the solace of a day's fishing on his own and he had recently given up squash and badminton to further this interest.

Alcohol was ever present in their house and visitors always mentioned their malt whisky optic in the kitchen. Money was not a problem. On his retirement ten years previously, George had taken advice from his Company's accountant and had a balanced portfolio of investments accruing from a lump sum retirement package together with two inheritances from their parents. Two cars adorned the double garage and a gardener, or rather, a handyman, spent three days per week keeping their acre of land spick and span. Judy also enjoyed the luxury of a housekeeper.

His annual re-election to the committees of the Horticultural Society, the Environmental Society and the Village Hall was automatic and he served all of them enthusiastically. The villagers expected him to organise fund raising events throughout the year for all three sections and he was not averse to subsidising less successful ventures out of his own pocket without detection. His car was always available for the less fortunate families in the neighbourhood to be transported to hospital or other urgent visits and the gardener was specifically nominated on the Insurance Policy as a named driver, mainly do those menial tasks.

Their mansion was lavishly furnished and there was no shortage of friends anxious to enjoy the comfort at the regular dinner parties. George always seemed to have something to celebrate. The greatest asset of the couple was that whilst they had unlimited finance, they never flaunted it. Although they were generous in their support of local charities, nobody could accuse them of buying their friendships. George had his own website and he prided himself with keeping a humorous story column updated for all to enjoy. Yes, it was fair to say that George and Judy were a much respected couple and very happy.

There was a shrill blast on a whistle.

"Ladies and gentlemen .... ladies and gentlemen, only 15 minutes left. If you want to make sure that you go home with these precious treasures at the right price, then you have only 15 minutes to place your bids. I'll blow again at 9.30 sharp, then ... no more bids."

George's voice, loud but friendly, was enough to command the attention of the villagers who had gathered in the village hall for a fund raising Silent Auction.

"Don't forget," he added, pausing for effect, "the roof above you won't last much longer. In fact, if it had been raining tonight, we would have had to carry all this stuff into the chapel room across the road. So please dig deep into your pockets and push up the prices. Oh! And by the way, if you see something really awful that has not got a bid on it, then put 50p in the name of one of your best friends!"

Gina, a newcomer to the village was a little perplexed and didn't join in the ensuing laughter. She confided to her next door neighbour that this was the first Silent Auction that she had attended and was surprised at the light-hearted seriousness of the whole affair. She could understand the interest in the Wedgwood and crystal pieces, but she was amazed that people had the nerve to put somebody else's name against the ghastly Victorian chamber pot in the corner.

"The first thing to remember," said her neighbour, "is that our Silent Auctions are not supposed to be silent. But because there is a prospect of the latest gossip, plus the fact that some people give us some pretty good items to auction, a good cross section of the village turns out on these evenings. Then there's George. He's pretty persuasive and we are lucky to have him in the village. He's very generous and gets everything moving."

She pointed towards a posse of the cricket team elbowed to the bar.

"There's another brainchild of the committee. The alcohol plays a dual role; it gets the men in here and the bidding always seems to gain momentum as the drink takes over. Look at Gerry on the left; he hasn't the faintest idea that he is leading in the bidding for the pot. Somebody has written "Jerry for Gerry" and that's the way it will stay until just before the end and then all hell will be let loose and the anti-bids, as we call them will mean that some poor bloke will end up paying about £6 or £7 for it. Nobody cares, just watch the rushing around when it gets near 9.30."

George boomed out again.

"There's a lot of chat going on, but not much else. Here's a bonus if you're quick. For the next thirty seconds, anybody my committee sees putting in an increased bid will get a chit for a free glass of wine. Only twelve minutes left, hurry."

"See what I mean ?" said Gina's neighbour, "as long as it brings in more money, nobody minds. If you have your eye on anything you had better watch out and make sure that you keep your name with the highest bid at the bottom of the slip of paper by each item that you're interested in."

The noise escalated by the minute; the bar hangers talked louder and faster and there was a crescendo of laughter as the punch lines of even more jokes of a Victorian vintage surfaced. The bidding moved up a gear. The enthusiasts, seeing that their last bids had been overtaken, now knew the extent of the interest and who was the opposition. The noise was continuous but the bidding was serious.

After twelve minutes the whistle went again.

"Five minutes more." The laughter was mixed with ribald comments about George's ancestry. But he knew how far to go without upsetting the stalwarts too much! He knew that it was well past 9.30 but whilst people were still prepared to plough more money into the village hall, why stop them? The activity grew even more intense. Pounds were added to the values before a long piercing blast on the whistle brought the bidding to an end.

"Stand clear of the tables, no more bidding." He waited for a lull in the noise. "You all know the rules, if your name is at the bottom of the cards by each item, then the item is yours, but not before you have paid the Treasurer and his mates over on these three tables. And we don't mind if you round your payments up, to the nearest pound."

The sudden swell of banter and shuffling bodies was interrupted once again.

"May I thank you all for turning up tonight. If you're honest enough to pay up, it looks as though we are in for a record tonight. And thanks to the ladies for providing the food."

"And a big hand to George for the wine," came the echo from a committee member.

Later that night in the grandeur of his six bedroom mansion, George ruminated over the evening's events. Having given himself the plaudits that it had been well organised, he lay with a satisfied smile, gazing at the ceiling.

"Seemed to go well, thanks to you, George. I didn't see the Turnbulls or the Scotts there. You'd think they would have made the effort, especially as they didn't give any auction items."

"Oh, I don't know," came the conciliatory reply. "They usually dip their hands into their pockets. They're coming on the French trip next month. The coach is full, by the way."

"That's just like you, always sticking up for people. That's why you're so popular. But that's one reason why I love you."

Never likely to miss an opportunity, George took his ever-loving Judy into his arms and sent her spiralling into the fields of happiness.

SANDRA

Sandra poured herself a second whisky and dry and settled down to end a rather hectic Sunday with two hours of Midsomer Murders. Weekends were usually uneventful, though seldom dull. Her apartment on the East Coast reflected the generosity of her lover sugar daddy and the extent of her rather extravagant lifestyle was never challenged by him, her neighbours, or the occasional lucky visitor invited to partake of her favours. Although she freely admitted to being in her late forties, Sandra had never married. Her nearest matrimonial brush had been successfully parried at the last minute when she realised that her freedom from the ensuing ties far outweighed the promised comfort of the attentive husband.

Sandra prided herself in her organisational abilities and whilst her insatiable appetite in bed meant taking risks to fill the voids when Maurice was not due to visit, she maintained a self-imposed discipline to ensure that doubts about her faithfulness were not aroused. Their relationship had always been on the understanding that no questions should be asked of each other regarding their commitments elsewhere, but from the moment that Maurice had funded the acquisition and furnishing of her new home, five years earlier, she had no intention of being caught rocking the boat. He was kind-hearted, attentive in the extreme and had never arrived unannounced. His prowess at love-making matched that of Sandra and the two of them spent hours sending each other into orbit. Being fifteen years younger than Maurice it was certainly in her interest to use her stamina to ensure that he remained a contented lover.

The whisky was refreshing and Sandra's attention moved from the plot on the TV to a recounting of the events of the past thirty six hours. It was unlike her to let Freddie monopolise her, but he had charmed her with an invitation to go to the races with the added attraction of the Hospitality Tent treatment. The Moet had flowed and the red carpet had extended to a gourmet evening meal followed by the inevitable beckoning of the hotel room. She grinned as she remembered Freddie's fumbling to get out of his trousers at speed and how they had fallen onto the floor trying to release his shirt that had got trapped in his fly zip. His ego was not the only thing to be deflated and Sandra had to take over and recharge his battery. But thereafter, Freddie had excelled himself and dawn had stretched to eleven am before they surfaced for brunch in the brasserie. Several hours later, it was with a measure of disappointment that she alighted from Freddie's car outside her own love nest. She couldn't remember having laughed so much for many months.

Although Maurice never visited her on a Sunday, Sandra was relieved to find no messages on the answer phone. He was not expected until early Tuesday morning but it was usual for him to ring if he wanted her to make any bookings. Tuesdays had started to become a habit for him in recent months and occasionally he even stayed overnight. Consequently, she ensured that the bed linen was changed on Mondays and she refrained from having other visitors until after Maurice's departure.

A third whisky, slightly larger, became a toy in her hand. As she twisted the stem she watched the wave-like line of alcohol swirl ever higher in the glass as her mind returned to Freddie. The CD player replaced the television and Verdi's Il Trovatore captivating rhythm filled the room. "What an amazing co-incidence," she thought. "The speed matched that of Freddie in full flight". Similarly, Verdi's Aida and Don Carlo reflected other stages of Freddie's performances. This was dangerous magic. Nobody, not even Maurice influenced her in this way.

The phone rang. Sandra let it ring four times whilst she steadied herself. Maurice must not detect the mood in which she had become entangled.

"Sandra, Freddie. Just couldn't get you off my mind. What a darling you've been. My machine keeps asking when it's going to happen again. Don't disappoint him. What do you say?"

"Calm it my warhorse." She grasped for words that would conceal a feeling of intense desire and would keep the options open.

"What were my last words to you? Freddie, a great weekend but I have commitments. Ring me on Thursday. I must go. Bye."

Poor Freddie. He had a lust for Sandra and the wherewithal to back it up. Sandra emptied the glass in one and threw herself backwards onto the sofa. "Come on, old girl," she sighed, "it's the drink. Off to bed. It will all clear itself in the morning."

Monday came and went. The apartment sparkled in anticipation of the benefactor's arrival and all naughty nuances that may otherwise cause concern, were hidden from sight, either by the duster or washing machine. The bathroom reeked of the French perfume given by Maurice on his previous visit and Sandra's lilac bathrobe concealed her latest purchase of undies. She selected a choice of his sportswear from his side of the wardrobe in case he arrived in a suit, whilst his blazer that he had to leave behind for cleaning following an Indian restaurant accident, was hanging prominently behind the bedroom door. Nothing was left to chance. Maurice was a stickler for detail and enjoyed the royal treatment that Sandra provided. She often wondered whether he expected, and received similar attention elsewhere, wherever that was, but she consoled herself with the assurance that he liked it and she would not disappoint him.

By the time that the doorbell sounded, his favourite breakfast of smoked salmon and scrambled eggs was ready to be cooked. Granary bread was perched on the toaster and the aroma of decaf filled the room.

"What would I do without you?" he smiled, as he swung her round in his arms. His ardour was, as usual, undisguised and with tongues and lips locked together, his warm hands deftly exposed her scantily clad welcoming body. Sandra responded with her own brand of handling and led him as if on a lead, to the awaiting bedroom.

Two hours later, as Maurice lay smiling in his sleep, Sandra slipped from his side and returned minutes later with the caffetiere and two brandies. A gentle kiss on his hairy chest brought him back to life but the attraction of the smell of coffee, for once, overtook the nearness of his beautifully tantalising mistress and he sat upright ready to receive the steaming cup.

"I have plans for us today. I hope you don't mind me springing this on you but I must go to Yorkshire. I thought we could stay overnight and get back in time for lunch tomorrow."

"Mind! I'd love to go" and without waiting to finish her coffee, she jumped off the bed and rummaged around in the wardrobe.

"What about this for this evening?" she called, waving a flimsy red suit with cream blouse. "Great, you look fantastic in anything."

JUDY

Judy had been playing way above her normal game lately and today was no exception. Her two playing partners in the Ladies Texas Scramble were enjoying every minute of the round. On three occasions Judy had rescued them from dropping shots and as the clubhouse beckoned, they were quietly confident that they may well get into the winning frame at the expense of some of the more fancied groups. As the rain greeted them on the 18th tee their cold fingers took over and the three drives were all off target. With her partners' second shots both well short of the green, Judy threw caution to the wind and despite the looks of horror on the faces of the watching pair, she discarded the recommended five iron and removed the cover from her number seven wood. She recalled George's oft repeated philosophy, "a decision is right, until proved wrong; have faith in it." Her faith was well-founded, though in a rather unexpected way. The ball was struck beautifully but slightly to the right. It got a complimentary kick forward from a bunker ridge from where it described a series of arcs from the edge of the green, over two conflicting undulations and while the threesome gazed in utter disbelief, the ball made its last trek to the base of the flag which gave a resounding thwack, hesitated and fell from view.

The ladies danced in uncontrollable glee. Judy was hugged and kissed in front of a galaxy of the early players watching from the warm security of the club lounge. The ensuing competition meal and presentation of the trophy and prizes was dominated by the congratulatory references to Judy and her team who had beaten the odds and carried off the gleaming cup and two of the three individual awards. By the time that the lady captain drew the celebrations to a close, the wine had taken its toll and Judy was in no state to drive home.

"George is away tonight on an offshore fishing do, so it looks like a taxi for me. I'll have to find a way of fetching the car tomorrow when he eventually comes home."

"I'll drive you home." Len was the latest in a long line of divorcees in the club. Members had remarked that there must be something in the water. To the best of Judy's knowledge, however, none of the recent splits was anything to do with affairs with other club members. Len's wife had deserted him six months earlier and Judy always found him polite and jolly.

"There you are," laughed Brenda, one of Judy's playing partners, "You've only got to sink a long putt and they all want to know you!"

"Well, if you're sure, but, I don't want to put you to any trouble. Can I buy you a drink before we go? That's daft. You're only taking me because I can't drive."

"Orange juice for me, brandy and ginger ale for you, yes?"

An hour later, with gentlemanly aplomb, Len held open the door of his Jag for his new companion. Judy sunk into the welcoming luxury and leant across to his side of the car and opened his door. She was conscious of the extent of thigh that was displayed by her action, but, what the hell! As he joined her, an arm encircled her and, amid giggles and wriggles, lips and tongues consummated the effects of a very satisfactory day on the course. Without any warning, Len broke free, fastened his safety belt, started the engine and aimed the car at speed towards the exit. Judy adjusted her skirt with a sigh, then allowed it to ride back, tantalisingly high. Neither spoke for several minutes.

"Your place or mine?" Again silence. Judy tried to regain her composure but she wasn't in control. For the first time since she had been married, temptation was staring her in the face. She had never wanted another man but here she was, knowing that in the next half hour, she would be at the mercy of a new lover, and she was looking forward to it.

"Yours" It was the safest bet. Without further words, the inevitable unfolded. The car sped into his driveway; the automatic doors of the garage opened at his command; Judy was helped from the warmth of the car, through a connecting door and into a spacious hallway, from which a spiral open-plan stairway beckoned. Len hesitated long enough to remove Judy's blouse and bra and steered her from behind on the upward journey to his sumptuous haven. Amidst a blur of alcohol and wanton lust, Judy was treated to an unprecedented experience of love and attention which even she, with all the wonderful knowledge from George's repertoire, realised was breaking new ground.

Evening became night. Night turned to dawn and their unabated passion stirred each other to greater heights until the utter exhaustion sent them both into dreamland, an entangled pair of warm bodies catapulted into oblivion.

Len was first to surface, regulated by his habit of always leaving home early to avoid road congestion on his way to work. Seeing the magic of his lovely companion, lying by his side, however, he made the immediate decision to forgo his work ritual and to extend the hospitality for this new-found blossom. Gentle caressing of her brow brought her close enough to the real world, for a semblance of a smile to enhance the beauty of her soft cheeks. He planted a lingering kiss on her forehead and whilst she gradually acquainted herself with her surroundings, he regained the role of lover and achieved the rhythm of the previous evening.

"Are we still going?" gasped Judy.

Len relaxed his grip of her soft back and rolled away.

"Darling" and after a brief pause, "just a morning call, breakfast will be served in a trice. Time for you to have a leisurely shower."

Scrambled egg and smoke salmon, orange juice and sparkling white wine, linen napkins and real coffee.

"The perfect compliment to a memorable twelve hours,"

"Not the last, I hope," said Len, reaching across the table and taking her hand and stroking the back with a tenderness not experienced by Judy for many years. Whilst George had always been attentive and a dab hand at surprises, perhaps he was taking her for granted lately. But, hang on, this is ridiculous.

"Steady the Buffs," she squeezed his hand, smiling. "You're a great guy in more ways than one, but I'm a happily married woman and you know only too well that George is a good husband to me. You, on the other hand have just returned to the market place and are a very attractive commodity. Let's leave you to the few available lady members. Don't think that I haven't enjoyed it. I have. But I'll kill you if this gets out."

Judy was immediately ashamed at her last comments but she needn't have worried. Len sided with her, promised her the immunity that she sought and offered to take her home.

Back in the security of her home, Judy sipped a large gin and tonic in the sunlit conservatory and recounted the events of the last twenty four hours. George would be proud to hear of her exploits on the course, but hell, enough said. Judy had never gone off the rails to such an extent. Both she and George had enjoyed an illicit snog at parties, but as far as she was concerned, there was never anything serious. She tried to console herself that this was a "one-off". George would be back from his fishing by lunchtime. She would cook him Toad in the Hole, his favourite.

But it was 3pm when he arrived and the Toad was cold, as was the reception he received. There was something about George that caused concern. He parked the car away from the house and carried his fishing tackle and case through the rear door. Judy watched him disappear into his study. Why was he carrying his blazer over his arm when she knew for a fact that he hadn't taken it with him yesterday?

"Have we got fish for supper?"

"No, they wouldn't bite. I had to give the only ones we caught to the boatman. I thought we'd go out for dinner tonight, if you like."

Judy sensed a distinct atmosphere between them but was determined not to feel guilty. Perhaps George had been on a date and was trying to cover it up. She bet to herself that his date had been small fry compared with her heated exchanges, but she had to put her secrets out of her mind. Whilst George indulged in a bath, Judy found herself going down the garden to look at the car. The reason for the distant parking was obvious. George was concealing a dent on the driver's door. But why hadn't he told her?

George lay back in the bath airing his limited operatic talents whilst he came to terms with his dilemma. If that stupid woman carried out her threats, he would need a story to cover up the fact that he was not alone when he accidentally cut across her at the roundabout. If he could prevent Judy from seeing the car for a day or so, a feasible yarn could be hatched. In hindsight, it would have been more sensible to have admitted responsibility at the time instead of blowing his top and trying to put the blame on the hapless lady. By refusing to exchange details, he had opened himself to all sorts of problems. The police may become involved if the lady wanted to press charges. There was no visible damage to her car, so his only hope was that she would swallow her pride and avoid the bother of getting into legal tangles.

George's first hurdle was overcome when Judy agreed to phone for a taxi to take them to the restaurant. They held hands throughout the journey and he listened attentively to Judy's tale of her prowess on the course. He chose to return to the subject several times during the meal, giving only fleeting anecdotes about his fishing. But when the coffee and brandies arrived, things started to go pear-shaped.

"What happened to your car?" No reply. George raised his glass.

"To my clever little Judy. Will you partner me in the Invitation Cup next month?"

"What happened to your car?"

"What happened? You mean the dent that some idiot put in the rear door? That was how I found it in the boat car park. I hope he did as much damage to his own car. Didn't even leave a note under the windscreen wiper."

Much to the relief of George, the subject was dropped and a second brandy revitalised the necessary organs. The taxi was hastily summoned, whisking them home to bed where both gave of their all; both fantasising over recent delicacies.

MAURICE

George hadn't intended to embark on a life of deceit. Just before he retired, he attended a pre-retirement course organised by his firm's Head Office in Suffolk. At the end of the third and last day a party was arranged in the local Swan Hotel and the wine flowed to excess. When the last of the guests had left, George got into conversation with a leggy, attractive lady, perched seductively on a bar stool. Her readiness to accept several drinks spurred him to greater things and his ego went into orbit when she agreed to follow him to his room in the hotel. It was only when she insisted on leaving at 2am that he discovered she was a prostitute, or, as she preferred, a professional lady. George paid her handsomely with conscience money, as he called it. He had never paid for sex before and begrudged it this time, but Sandy impressed him as being someone different.

Whilst having breakfast next morning, he received a call from her, asking him to visit her before he left town. She emphasised that there were no strings attached and she wanted to thank him for his generosity. Without considering the ramifications of his actions, he drove to a small block of town houses on the outskirts and found her blowing a kiss through the curtains of her apartment. She opened the door dressed in a see-through housecoat which she loosened as he entered. There followed three hours of unabated lust. Both gave of their best until she drew the session to a close.

George left with her card and a promise that she would give him pride of place if he chose to return.

Two weeks into his retirement, George found himself thinking of Sandy, or Sandra as her card called her. Gradually, he hatched a plan whereby he could return to Suffolk, announcing that he was setting up a consultancy. Naturally it would entail a deal of travelling. Judy had never involved herself in the detail of his work and took even less interest in the financial side of their marriage. She was comfortable in their arrangements and enjoyed her freedom which she had to admit was far superior to the marriage ties of her many friends.

George and Sandra's relationship took root and within two months he had acquired a more luxurious place for her. It was when he handed the keys of the property to her that he laid the ground rules of retaining their own security of past actions without disclosure. Whilst he would own the property, she could look upon it as being hers and could entertain as she wished. He asked only that she would welcome him whenever he gave her notice of his intention to visit.

The dual personality became a challenge and he found himself establishing a second identity in Suffolk. Sandra knew from the outset that his name was Maurice. He had changed his initials round and dropped the Mc from his surname. A photocopy of his birth certificate, suitably altered to reflect these changes, had been sufficient to open an account with the local bank manager who he had met at the nearby golf club. With his low handicap, he had no difficulty getting his membership confirmed at the club.

As he travelled between his two homes, he planned the expansion of his interests. The challenge, the excitement, the thrills of the near misses and most of all, the enhanced sex activity, all contributed to his overall objective of living to reach the age of one hundred and five, a target set during his pre-retirement course. He accepted that the journey from Kent, his natural home, and Suffolk, took two and a half hours but the advantages had to be measured in the limited chances of being caught red-handed. Sandra certainly welcomed the increasing interest shown by Maurice. She loved being spoilt.

The one area that gave George a tingling in his conscience, was his activities in the church at his Kent home. As a member of the Parochial Church Council he was held with great respect by the Rector and the parishioners and he volunteered often when a reader of the scriptures was required. He declined approaches made for him to join the choir on the pretext that God deserved better. He admitted to himself that his dual roles made him a hypocrite, but excused himself in the knowledge that the person who had not sinned, had not yet been born, well, not for two thousand years.

He looked upon his relationship with Judy as being rock solid. It hadn't been like that for all the thirty five years of marriage, but he prided himself in managing to placate Judy for the ten years preceding his retirement, by not having, nor wanting, an affair that would have jeopardised their stability. Neither of them had fallen out of love with each other, but both had strayed; in the case of George it was out of bravado rather than from boredom. After the birth of their only child, a daughter, George had felt a trifle lonely amidst the home chores and had unwittingly sought solace in the arms of a workmate. Tongues had wagged and George had been humiliated by Judy in the presence of the rector.

Later, after their daughter had started school, Judy had a mild fling with an admirer. George had suspected it immediately and, when challenged, Judy blamed the fact that she had joined the 60% of lonely housewives who were just sitting at home waiting for somebody to tell her that her hair looked great. Both affairs blew over without festering, mainly because both parties had too much to lose at the time.

As the weeks of his relationship with Sandra turned into months, George's confidence grew. He enjoyed demonstrating his repertoire of jokes and general knowledge with the very receptive Sandra who in turn, responded with her appreciation of dealing with a mature and experienced bed mate. Life had taken on a new meaning and challenge and George was revelling in it. He went out of his way to make Judy feel really wanted, by increasing the frequency of gifts of flowers and chocolates and by dining out more regularly. He threw himself into his village activities with added gusto. At the same time he looked upon the Suffolk outings as an opportunity to relax mentally. At first he had planned his excursions on a weekly basis, but with his increased successes, he began to think ahead and drop gentle hints at home that in addition to his fishing jaunts, his consultancy would require overnight stays in the near future.

One such venture culminated in taking Sandra to Yorkshire. Although he had made tentative bookings for the pair of them, he had not warned her of the pending escapade. This would be their first away-day and night and he wanted to tread carefully. He also wanted to be in control of events without Sandra having the opportunity to inject her own expectations. The surprise of going to Yorkshire was marked by Sandra's excitement throughout the two days. She stroked her partner's leg whilst he was driving, something he had never experienced. She laughed at his stories and complimented him on his choices at the dinner table, in front of the hotel staff who obviously assessed the relationship at a glance and acted accordingly. The King-sized four poster bed was a hit and their exploits reflected the added thrill.

The "fly in the ointment" was the brush with the lady driver just outside York. George had acted rather brazenly in front of Sandra, but immediately regretted his stupidity, not only because of the lady's threat to inform the police, but also the fact that the event subdued him, giving Sandra an insight of another side of him. On his homeward journey to Kent, George gave himself a severe talking to, reminding himself of the unnecessary risk that he had generated.

"If only I had stopped to think."

VOICES

"I'll get it. I'm by the bedroom phone." Judy noticed the urgency of her own insistence. Surely it couldn't possibly be Len. He wouldn't risk it. Or would he? In the split second of the initial ring something told her to get to the phone first and having achieved the objective, her anxiety affected her normal confidence.

"Hello," was the only word that escaped. Silence. Was he there, waiting for his own nerve to take over. "Hello." Judy's tone became more demanding. Perhaps he was reclining on that soft warm bed, suddenly tongue tied. A click denoted the end of the call and she replaced the receiver with a sigh of relief. Whoever it was had backed off or got the wrong number, but Judy sat on the bed, poised, ready to pounce if the caller had rehearsed their opening words.

Downstairs in the lounge, George had fallen over a chair in his haste to reach the phone. Every call that day had the marked possibility of being from the Yorkshire Constabulary and he needed to intercept their enquiries. Judy's voice indicated that his fears were unfounded on this occasion and he lost interest in the call and the subsequent ringing a few minutes later.

Judy, however, couldn't have worked faster and grabbed the instrument before the opening double ring had completed.

"Judy McRoberts." Her voice had regained its normality.

"Oh, I didn't know what name to expect. My name is Grace Millbank."

Judy didn't recognise the voice. "Did you want to speak to my husband?"

She called downstairs for George to take over. It was only after George had boomed his name at the unsuspecting lady, that Judy replaced her extension. But as she did so, Judy felt sure that the opening words of the unknown voice had been related to his car. She daren't retrieve the receiver because George would have detected the click, so she moved to the head of the stair well to listen. Unfortunately, George had closed the lounge door and she would have to rely on his explanation. As she waited for George's appearance, Judy recognised the sudden change in her own attitude.

One minute she was in fear of receiving an illicit call from an admirer and the next, she was doubting her husband's honesty.

"Anything special?" Judy asked casually, over dinner.

"Oh no, I might be hearing about who caught my car. But I'm not too hopeful. I've only got part of the number from a bystander."

The matter was dropped but not without Judy noticing that George was unusually tetchy. Over the course of the next few days there were three more unexplained calls and Judy became more and more suspicious. But the tables were turned suddenly when George took yet another incoming call and calmly announced that her boyfriend wanted to speak to her. Knowing it to be a false alarm did nothing to stop her temperature rising and she could feel her face reddening.

"Judy here, can I help?"

"Hi there, Len Bishop here. Is it OK to speak? If not I can ring back."

"Yes, of course it is," stuttered Judy, composing herself for another shock.

"Well, can I count on you for the mixed pairs in a few weeks time?" I hear that you don't usually partner your husband and I'd love to see you again."

Judy froze, made an excuse of needing her diary and ran upstairs. Looking in the mirror and adjusting her hair gave her the required boost of confidence and returned to the conversation in a perky mood.

"Love to, that's settled then. Will you do all the admin? I'll expect you to carry me through to the final."

"I can't believe what I'm hearing. Yes to everything. I'll carry you anywhere. Gosh, I can't believe, er, I'll let you know the details." He rang off.

George met her in the lounge.

"Was that the pairs you were arranging? I was hoping to partner you myself. I like playing with a winner. Can't you change it?"

"No and I don't want to either. Fancy Len Bishop wanting to play with me, of all people."

"That's not all he'll be after. Mark my words."

George went outside, swallowing his pride and chastising himself for trying to create a scene. He was in no position to point the finger. Wait until he had cleared up all of his own cliff-hanger before he pushed his luck. Anyhow, if the pairing proved to be successful, then surely there would be more travel opportunities. George felt better already. Christ, the phone was ringing.

Unable to face another crisis so soon, Judy let it ring. She heard the door slam and an expletive from George as he dropped the phone in his haste to answer it. Judy remained static on the landing, trying to control a pending sneeze.

"Yes, I was the driver." Pause. "No, she wasn't. My wife said nothing."

The lounge door closed and the spying ceased. Judy sat on the edge of her bed, pondering over the grains of the sinister episode. "So there was a lady with him! What was he up to? No wonder he didn't want to be drawn on the affair. That's what it is. He's having an affair, right under my nose."

Judy thought long and hard. What a day this was turning out to be and both of them were entertaining voices of intrigue. 'We're as bad as each other,' she thought, 'but I've got more to gain by lying doggo.' The thought of Len gave her a warm feeling in her groin. What a charmer! Wait until the girls find out about their pairing for the mixed.

George had obviously benefited from his call. His smile returned and his love for Judy resumed its normal mantle. He put his arm round her waist and pulled her to him, kissing her quite wildly. Judy reacted with her normal fervour but as they lay in each other's arms after an unusually long session, it was not George who was at the forefront of Judy's thoughts. It was not George who had driven her to her passionate extremes. But George was content. His performance had, in his opinion, been quite commendable.

"I fancy a dinner party. What about you?"

VILLAGE GOSSIP AND CONCERN

The afternoon of the party brought nothing but disharmony to the couple and Judy had longed for the guests to ring, cancelling their visit. She knew in her heart that this could never happen but George had been intolerable all day. There had been no more devious phone calls but something had upset him and he found fault with all her plans. Her choice of lamb shanks was wrong because she had bought imported lamb. The melons to accompany the prawns were the wrong shape and colour. The broccoli and stilton soup was not home made. The raspberry pavlova was over-cooked.

Now it was her turn. George had reluctantly agreed to look after the dining table setting and the drinks department. But as she put her head round the corner of the dining room, she let loose her fury.

"That's the wrong table cloth. I told you to use the cream linen to off-set the red flower arrangement. I also said that pre-drinks should be in the conservatory, not over there in the alcove. And why have you put my place card next to your boring fart on the village hall committee. He's your guest, in fact, they are all your guests, so just put me by Eve and then, at least, I can have some girl talk. We can discuss you and your fancy piece who was with you in the car in York."

George's face contorted with a rage. Judy had never seen such anger in him before. She took a step back in astonishment as he yanked the tablecloth from its moorings sending glasses and cutlery in all directions. He strode out of the room without a word and minutes later she heard gravel fly from the driveway as his car sped away.

Judy was shell-shocked and stood motionless for several minutes, trying to take in the devastation. Glass and salt had reached the corners of the room and the aroma of mint sauce permeated the air. Her stunned silence turned to self pity and she collapsed, crying, in a heap on the floor, narrowly missing a jagged segment.

The hall clock striking five brought her to her senses and she got to her feet and sought refuge in the kitchen. Fortunately, nothing was spoiling in that department and she checked the recipe book for the seafood sauce that was yet to be prepared. Suddenly, George appeared at the door of the kitchen, as quickly as he had disappeared.

"Thought better of it," he muttered, sheepishly. "Daft going off like that. Everything seems to have gone pear-shaped today. Can I climb back on board ?"

"Might as well. Somebody will have to eat this lot, if we cancel. Though I don't know why I'm bothering at all."

Judy realised that she had gained the high ground and must keep it.

"You can start by clearing up that mess and doing things the way that I had suggested in the first place. And you'd better not step out of line tonight."

George was taken aback by Judy's authoritative tone. It was most unusual, perhaps understandable in the circumstances, but he didn't like it. He set about picking up the largest pieces of glass and rescued the tablecloth which he took into the garden and shook violently. The vacuum cleaner was put to work and in half an hour, the preparations for the party had been restored, but at a price that George would have preferred to have avoided. As he showered, he ruminated over his mismanagement of the whole affair since the knock in the car. His cover-up was not working and he could feel Judy on his trail. He had to admit to himself that he was losing his touch.

Despite the analysis of his dilemma and his intention to apply caution throughout the evening, he could not have prepared himself for the sequence of events that Judy had planned for him. The reception and first two courses of the meal had followed the normal pattern of their entertaining, with George holding the stage and ensuring that the guests were being plied with ample alcohol. Judy, however, refrained from having top-ups after the initial glass with the main course and George should have noticed the signs. But as usual, he kept his own glass full and his stories got louder and coarser, until he made an unfortunate choice of yarn about a commercial traveller with his secretary in York. Judy pounced.

"That's a bit close to home, isn't it George?" Then after a pause whilst the guests listened to the surprise interruption, she continued. "Come on George, you know a bit about visiting York with strange women in your car. We are in for a true story tonight. George will now fill us in and tell us who he had on board when he crashed his car in York."

The silence was broken by the rector who sensed an atmosphere developing and started to tell of a visit to the Minster two years previously. Judy persisted and reminded George of the several conversations with the phantom caller who must have been involved.

"You remember, don't you George?" she chided.

George left the room, not to be seen again during the meal. Revitalised by her daring, Judy played the perfect host for the cheese course and coffee, ably assisted by Eve whose knowing winks and dextrous carrying of the dirty crockery, enabled Judy to concentrate on the drinks trolley. The guests acted as one would expect in such a situation and in the space of a half hour from serving coffee, Judy was at the front door saying goodnight to rector who was the last to leave. No sooner had she shut the door, George crashed through the kitchen door, blood streaming down his face.

"Don't ask me, I just don't know," was all that George kept repeating. "I heard a car door slamming and found that I was lying in a pool of blood."

Judy's natural nursing instincts, coupled with a degree of guilt took over and George was hustled to a chair and the bathing began, accompanied by a glass of scotch from the optic. "We'll see what it looks like in the morning. Now, off to bed."

Morning disclosed the source of the bleeding. Judy rose early, to find segments of the tumblers shaken from the tablecloth during their argument the previous evening. It was probable that George's head had caught the step by the garage as he fell amongst the splinters. Armed with this discovery, Judy took a pot of tea to the bedroom, only to find George on the phone to the doctor, asking for an appointment for him to look at his elbow that had swollen drastically.

"Ok doctor," said George obediently, "I'll get Judy to run me down straight away."

Church was given an almost unprecedented miss. In fact, after the couple had been absent for three Sundays in a row, villagers sensed that something was going wrong. Two parishioners who had been at the dinner party, reported that George had looked stressed throughout the evening and the couple had obviously been arguing. As the rumours spread round the village, the exaggerated story was that George had been caught red-handed by Judy, having an affair.

The rumour mongering came to a head at a village Bridge Party attended by the Rector where he overheard the doctor's wife referring to a visit by George to her husband's surgery, with a painful elbow. The swollen forehead and George's flushed appearance had caused the doctor to quiz him and send him for a check up. The Rector decided that a visit was necessary and was concerned to find the couple completely distressed. George told of his surgery visit and said that within an hour of arriving there, he had been hustled away to the Grove Hospital neurology department, for a scan. George had then waited daily for the results and had only just arrived back home having spoken at length to the doctor. George's voice was almost inaudible.

"Apparently I've got a malignant tumour in a part of the head that makes an operation impossible."

With long pauses between sentences, George gave the unbelievable prognosis that he must get used to the fact that he would be dead by June. The tumour had been present for a long time, but the fall had aggravated it. Judy stayed silent, staring out of the window.

The Rector hesitated, searching for the correct thing to say. He was not normally at a loss for words but, somehow, this was not an ordinary situation. Here was a man who could not be moved from his attitude to life, certain that it would go on for ever at the same pace as he had enjoyed since retirement. Now he appeared broken, without hope and with death coming towards him. The Rector needed to play for time. He must not be seen to be sharing the hopelessness of the situation, but he must go away and return with a positive approach. He encouraged them to hold hands with him and to pray for help, to find guidance and hope. Then he left, promising to return later that day and to see if they could plan ahead, jointly.

To his absolute amazement, when he returned, George and Judy were smiling and brandishing whisky glasses. He was hustled into the lounge where a sherry awaited him. George couldn't stop talking excitedly about their plans. Apparently, immediately the Rector had left them after the prayers, Judy had solved the problem. She remonstrated with George, reminding him that he was all-powerful and that nothing worried him. Why shouldn't he prove the experts wrong? Why should they sit long faced? The enthusiasm had been catching and within minutes, the two of them were dancing to Kenny Ball.

The Rector collected his thoughts quickly and joined in the celebrations. Here was a couple planning initially for six months to do a host of travelling to places that they had wanted to see, but had not yet fitted into their busy lives. Well, there hadn't been any need to rush. Judy had always refused to fly which created a small problem. But what was wrong with a world cruise? George had already surfed the internet for opportunities and the evidence was on the table.

"Yes, we're leaving with Jenny our daughter in three days time. That gives me just about enough time to sort out all our jobs. Luckily, all our inoculations are in order and I've some pills. The complete itinerary will remain fluid, depending on our enjoyment of each place."

The villagers gave them a good send-off, everyone putting on a brave face, secretly fearing that George may not return, but admiring them for their courage. The sceptics thought that too much pressure had been put on Judy, looking after him every second of the day in strange countries. But such was the strength of the couple.

THE WHEEL OF FORTUNE

Nothing was heard from George for six weeks, during which time the gardener and cleaner did what was necessary to maintain the property in good order. Then a bout of cards arrived, allaying all fears for George's safety. Nobody wanted to read between the lines.

Another two weeks of silence was followed by more cards. This was George at his best. "What problem?" You could almost hear him saying the words, just like the old George. People began looking at the calendar, ticking the weeks. Surely, Judy must be doing the same thing? April slipped into May and the world had swallowed up the travellers. "No news is good news" became the essence of all conversations in the village and even the Rector's sermon took on the theme that the parishioners were in safe hands.

Then, unexpectedly, George arrived home in a taxi, closely followed by the doctor's car. The gardener greeted them but left them to enter the house alone.

"I'm glad you travelled back so quickly George. Judy and Jenny OK I hope?"

"Yes, I left them in Aukland. What's all this about?"

With an arm round him, the doctor guided George to a sofa and calmly announced that there had been a terrible error at the hospital and that George had been given the wrong results and prognosis.

"So, you're not going to die. You'll get your century after all."

George's stunned silence gave an eerie atmosphere to the room. The explanation of how it may have happened went unheard and George sat motionless for what seemed to be an eternity.

"I feel sick," he said and left the room, leaving the doctor to ruminate over his own choice of words. Fifteen minutes later George returned, red-eyed, apologising for the delay. Grasping the malt whisky he invited the doctor into the conservatory and immediately went on the offensive.

"Doc, you ought to know that the news I received at the hospital shattered me and I'm convinced that nobody can have any idea of the mental suffering that I've endured since that visit. I doubt whether I will ever really recover my nonchalant attitude to life again." Having paused for what seemed to be an eternity, he added, "so I will be taking the Health Authority "to the cleaners". A lesser man may have taken his own life rather than face the death sentence."

The doctor could see the financial plan unfolding in front of him and he questioned his own part in the episode. As George had stated, he wasn't interested in the money, but others should be protected against such inefficiency. At this point, George dropped his bombshell.

"On second thoughts I'm now even more determined to benefit from my second chance of achieving longevity and to make one or two changes in my lifestyle at the same time. Consequently, I'll retract the veiled threat to sue, if you agree to ensure that this news remains personal and unpublished within the village, or to Judy. This will give the appearance that I'm beating the odds of survival. Perhaps you can prescribe a year's supply of some innocuous pills that would assist in giving credence to my renewed confidence."

The doctor considered the devious plan and saw no breach of ethics, except in that he also had an allegiance to Judy. But a husband was entitled to privacy, even in medical situations, so on the face of it, the passage of time would blur the detail. After all, it was George who had suffered weeks of terror and his planned little bouts of one-upmanship could compensate. The two men shook on the deal and the doctor agreed to secure confidentiality from his own staff.

Meanwhile, the gardener lost no time in spreading the news that George had returned alone. The Rector who was one of the first to hear, undertook to check on his well-being.

"So you see Rector, the great news is that there is a new drug available that will give me at least another six months. Judy and I can carry on with our tour as planned."

"That's great news. Our prayers have been answered. Well done. I'll leave you and spread the good tidings."

George felt smug that he had overcome his first hurdle by hoodwinking the Rector. Judy was delighted but not surprised with the news of the drug discovery and suggested that George should enjoy a few days with his friends before attempting the return journey. Having agreed, reluctantly, he wished her well, telling her that if she decided to go on extended trips, then she should leave a forwarding note at the hotel.

George then put phase one of his second chance to achieve longevity into place. He packed his golf clubs, fishing tackle and a large case of clothes into the car. He was about to make his traditional phone call to Suffolk from his office when he realised that he was holding Judy's mobile. His curiosity was aroused immediately, by the number of text messages from "L". Most gave news about the golf club and George remembered that Judy had intended to partner Len in a competition. However, one comment made him delve further and George went to the pile of unopened mail in the lounge and searched for the letter to Judy containing a fixture list. This meant opening several likely pieces before he found, to his horror, a handwritten note pinned to the Ladies Section fixtures for the following season. Len and Judy were having an affair.

The call to Suffolk was received by a screech of delight from Sandra, but this did not make the journey any easier. George's imagination ran riot and he found himself shouting obscenities about Judy's unfaithfulness and castigating her for daring to challenge his own activities. His self pity led to more scheming and by the time his destination came into sight, George had formed a most outrageous plan of revenge.

.   A romantic evening was followed by a week of ecstatic philandering with scarcely a spare moment to talk coherently about the future. Ten days after his arrival in Suffolk, he left a message at Judy's hotel that he would be away for a week with chums. At the end of that week, George spoke to her from a hotel in Pitlochry, saying that he felt more relaxed about his condition and would fly to Auckland in three days time, having secured an airline reservation. In the meantime he intended to go fishing on the Loch the next day, but would welcome a call from her when convenient.

His next outing was to Perth where he sold his car and, from a different dealer he bought a 4 x 4, which he parked in a secluded copse close to Loch Tummel and walked the couple of miles back to his hotel. During the evening he disclosed to the Proprietor that his wife may phone from New Zealand and that, as he had arrived by train, he would hire a car, boat and fishing tackle for two days.

George's plans were just about to materialise. Towards the end of the first day, he rowed towards the centre of the deserted loch where he jettisoned the tackle, together with his hat and one oar. He then made for the shore, close to where his 4 x 4 car was parked. Two hundred yards from land, he abandoned the boat containing his coat, wallet, old credit cards, airline booking and Judy's details and swam to the desolate shore. A change of clothes awaited him in his car and with a smug smile of satisfaction, he set off on his journey to the rest of his new life.

It was not all plain sailing, however, evidenced by the shock when he saw in the national press two days later that the man presumed drowned in Loch Tummel had been named, following the tracing of his family who had been touring New Zealand. Suicide had not been ruled out. The thought of the anguish that he had put on Judy brought a lump into his throat and it was days before he came to terms with it. But life had to go on. Growing a beard and restyling his hair helped to change the image, especially as he began indulging in a more hectic round of socialising with his more beautiful and much younger lady companion. Frequently he found his thoughts drifting to his former home, family and activities, but he dismissed them in the cause of ambition.

Then, a greater shock hit him one evening whilst driving through Kent on his way to a business appointment. His car radio picked up the local "What's on in the County" programme and to his amazement, he learnt that there would be a thanksgiving service for the life of the man who had presumably drowned in Scotland the previous month. It would take place at 8pm the following evening at St. Mary's Church in his old village.

George pulled into a lay-by, feeling sick. His brain raced through the maze of actions that he had provoked and the ordeal that Judy must be suffering. Losing the appetite for his engagement, George went directly to the hotel where he had intended to stay overnight after his meeting. Throughout the night he wrestled with his conscience, changing plans by the minute. He couldn't go back, he knew that. But there was something tugging at him. By morning, his doubts had gone, replaced by an injection of egoism. His mind was made up. He would listen to his own obituary. All day, he alternated between bravado, sheer cunning and stupidity in an endeavour to satisfy this challenge. By early evening he was on his way, along the coast road, putting the final touches to his devious plan. He would slip into the church early and hide in the bell ringers' loft. Whilst he would have no view of the people, he could sit in comparative comfort and listen to the inevitable plaudits.

The congregation filled the tiny church and one by one, well-wishers gave anecdotes about his past, tearfully reminding his family of the extent of love that they had enjoyed with these villagers. Judy sat with Jenny in the front pew surrounded by fellow golf club members. Both were moved by the sincerity of the many contributors. Finally, the Rector summed up the feelings of George's friends by referring to George's main ambition of becoming a centurion.

"George, with all his great qualities towards his fellow men and his love for his family, unfortunately had one lasting failure. He ignored the part that God plays in the allocation of Luck in our lives."

Three days later, Judy was reading a report of the Memorial Service in the County newspaper. It referred to the glowing tributes to a community-minded man. 'George would have loved to have heard the service,' she thought and then she glanced casually at a story in an adjacent column.

"An unidentified man fell to his death when his 4x4 car skidded from the road near Beachy Head on Tuesday afternoon. The police are not treating the incident as suspicious."

I'M DYING TODAY

At a time when the world's press was punctuated with news, or the lack of news about hostages, my grandson was engaged in church work in Africa. Groups who took hostages for cash or political recognition cared nothing for the family stress or the value of life in general.

I marvelled at the resilience of those prisoners who controlled their emotions in such circumstances and wondered how I might react. I'm sure that the following verse comes nowhere near the heart-searching, that a hostage, facing the inevitable, would encounter.

FACING DEATH

I'm going to die today.

It isn't my decision; I never chose the date.
It's been decided for me; just put it down to fate.
It's not because it's raining or I got told off at work,
I've not been made a bankrupt or associated quirk.
My days were never boring; I'm not fed up with life
I had no inclinations to stab an erring wife.
I saw a need in Africa, the children there to aid,
But then became a hostage, until a ransom's paid.

I'm going to die today, what will I miss ?

I've been locked up for ages and have come to grips with death
I cry no more, my tears were shed with every dying breath.
I've said farewell, expressed regret for misdemeanours done
And thought of all those little things that gave me so much fun.
My family, friends and workmates; the gifts that nature gave
The sun, the rain, the flowers, to join me on my grave.
The faculties God gave me, for sight, sound, smell and touch,
The country walks that used them, that added joy, so much.

I'm going to die today. What a waste.

My captors came to see me this morning just at dawn
They sat two hours beside me, they both had daggers drawn.
One spoke about his children in need of nourishment
The dire straits of his family, unless the cash was sent.
It's all a vicious circle. I told him of my son
Who came with me to Africa to see God's work is done.
He carries water daily to ease the village needs
And helps the stricken families with necessary deeds.

I'm going to die today. I don't want to.

The look upon the captor's face was sullen and complexed.
I knew my cause was hopeless and guessed what would come next.
It wasn't their decision, they wanted me to know.
In six hours they would come for me, the time for me to go.
I prayed so hard my brain went numb, my eyes began to nod
The hour was getting closer; I made my peace with God.
Then footsteps clattered up the path to end my final day.
I heard the keys turn in the lock. And then they went away.

I'm NOT going to die today ….

NOCTURNAL HAPPINESS

"Night is generally my time for walking."
That is how Charles Dickens started his "Old Curiosity Shop". Surely, I can conjure up a tale to expand that beginning.

My mind went back to my childhood evacuation to Blagdon in Somerset, the background to my published book, "A Stranger And Afraid". This is a superb walking area, being one of the prettiest spots in England. In common with all boys, I was susceptible to rumours of intrigue in the village, when all strangers were possible spies. It added to the spice of growing up in a time of upheaval.

Writers, fortunately, grant themselves the authority to expand on the truth, as my story reveals.

NOCTURNAL HAPPINESS

Night is generally my time for walking. In Summer I often leave home early in the morning and roam about the fields and lanes all day, or even escape for days or weeks together.

One night I happened to be walking in one of my favourite haunts in the Mendip Hills area of Somerset. Earlier in the day I had pitched my tent in a field that I remembered as 'Weaver's Patch' from my childhood. I had set off on my walk in the direction of Priddy in the afternoon, hoping to reach the summit of Blackdown, the highest point of the Mendips, after dark. The weather forecast had promised a clear sky, so I was prepared to enjoy the delight of seeing the distant illuminations indicating the small town of Cheddar to the south, Weston-super-Mare and Clevedon twenty five miles to the north west and a massive area of bright sky over Bristol, eighteen miles to the north, hidden behind the range of hills near its airport.

I had removed my back-pack that contained my supper and stood, feet apart, in ecstasy as I peed against the monument depicting the summit of Blackdown. I was about to give the regimental three or four shakes before tucking him away for the evening, when I detected a presence.

"Can someone hear me?" The quiet voice of a lady came from the path behind me. "I know you're there. Please help me."

With one hand hiding my manhood I extracted a torch from my pocket. The beam pierced the darkness and silhouetted a young lady attired in an orange florescent rain jacket. My first thoughts were for my own safety. She, obviously, would not be alone, but where was her accomplice? Why would anyone be up on the hill? They couldn't possibly expect to find a person to rob on Blackdown at 10pm. Suppose she really was alone, how did she get there? My free hand checked that my pecker had been secured in the pants, before braving the situation. Drawing alongside the lady, I offered her my hand.

"Hi, I'm Gerald, how can I help?"

"Sounds daft I know, but I'm lost. I shouldn't be." She ignored the hand of friendship. "I know Blackdown inside out but I've lost all sense of direction. I must have missed the path to Hamm. It was probably when I tripped and found myself walking over whortleberries instead of walking on a path. I expected to be home by nine. I know that I've been climbing but I don't recognise the spot."

"Well, you're an hour late already. You must have walked miles out of your way and now you're at the top. Where are you heading?"

"Hamm Cottage at the top of Burrington Coombe."

"Know it well. When I lived here fifteen years ago, the old Simmonds couple lived there."

"They died and the Langers have lived there ever since."

It was then that I began to smell a rat. How could she get lost if she knew the area so well? It had been a hot day and the evening air was still pleasantly warm. So why did she sport a rain jacket? As I was about to point her in the direction of the main path, she diverted the conversation.

"What brings you to this desolate place at this time of night? Surely you're not lost?"

I started to explain that, as a night hawk, I enjoyed the freedom of loneliness, which enabled me to gaze at the wonders of space. I turned to pick up my pack, intending to invite her to sit and share my supper, but to my amazement, in that flicker of an eyelid, she had disappeared. I called but there was no response.

With the exception of that intrusion, my evening passed uneventfully. As I approached my field, I thought I saw a badger, and that was the last thing that I would like, rummaging through my things at night. But there was a night visitor. When I awoke, I found a note pinned to the tent flap.

'Please pay camp fee at Hamm House on Cheddar Road.'

I breakfasted in a confused state. This field had always been Weaver's'.

What a coincidence that I should have chosen to camp on a spot Belonging to the strange lady who had entered my life on Blackdown. Why didn't she wake me if she wanted money? The intriguing situation got the better of me and I decided to delay my walk until I had found some answers. The only way that this could be achieved would be to go and pay my dues.

A milk float drawn by a tired-looking nag was passing the field as I slammed the gate shut.

"Morning. Did you get my note? I didn't want you to waste your time calling at the farm."

That answered one question. It wasn't the lady who had called.

"Oh. So you left it. Are you from the farm? You used to own this field when I was a boy."

The ensuing chat told me that this man was the son of old Weaver that I had known. The father had been approached by the owner of Hamm Cottage, Carl Langer, who wanted to buy the barn and field. The price offered had been too good to refuse.

Rumours had surrounded the Langers from the moment that they moved into Hamm Cottage in 1938. He made a fortune during the war but nobody knew how. He had disappeared from the area for the last year of the war and the local constable hinted that it had something to do with being interned as an alien because his parents were German.

The most damning accusation against him was that he had been a spy. In 1941 a decoy, simulating Bristol marshalling yards had been erected on Hamm Common, on the opposite side of Burrington Coombe from Hamm Cottage. The success of the decoy meant that for three weeks the common had been blasted by German bombers sent to attack Bristol. Suddenly, the deception ceased. The lights failed to operate. The army found that the control block had been infiltrated and equipment had been stolen. Subsequently, Bristol was pounded for many consecutive nights until the blitz ceased. The finger of suspicion for the thefts was pointed at Carl. Unknown people were seen entering Hamm Cottage at night and rumours escalated. Villagers acting as Air Raid Wardens made regular visits on the pretext of checking blackout systems, or hid in the garden trying to refute or confirm stories of people hearing morse code tappings. But nothing happened to satisfy the rumour mongers.

When Carl returned to Hamm Cottage he had apparently remarried, but the couple were not accepted as friends

"The trouble really came to a head ten years ago." The farmer was in full flow, enjoying injections of his own suppositions of what might have happened.

"Carl overheard a conversation between two villagers in The Bull, discussing the Langers during the war. There was a bit of fisticuffs but the outcome was that two weeks later, one of the villagers disappeared. After several raids on Hamm Cottage, the villager was found buried in the barn in your field. Carl got fifteen years. I suppose he'll be out soon."

"What happened to his wife?"

"She's another strange one. Ever since she arrived here, I know of nobody who has ever spoken to her. She doesn't shop in the village, but is sometimes seen out walking, mainly at night."

I'd heard enough to convince me that I ought to return to my tent and think about my next move. A shudder went through my body as I glanced at the barn. The camping fee was the least important thing on my mind. Did I want to spend another night there? Moving camp would be a bind and I intended to see so much more in the area. 'What the hell', I thought, 'I'll think about it as I walk.'

The walk, however didn't solve anything. The pleasure of walking in the Mendips always clears the mind of any problems. A lunchtime pint in Burrington followed by a climb behind Shipham meant an early evening stroll back over Blackdown, bringing me back home for a fry-up. To my amazement, after leaving the hill path and approaching the road bordering my field, I came face to face with the lady who had become the centre of my experiences. At first, I thought that she was going to pass without speaking. She seemed to be in a world of her own.

"Hello," I ventured, "not lost today?"

She jumped, visibly surprised at my presence.

"Oh sorry, I didn't ..." The sentence remained unfinished.

"I'm camping in Weaver's Patch, your field with the barn. I owe you some money."

"Nobody else pays, so why should you?"

And she was gone, into the evening gloom.

The following morning, the sun woke me early and I found myself mulling over the strange sequence of events: two meetings with Carl's wife; the stories of the farmer; the aggro of the villagers against Carl and everyone's indifference towards his wife. And the barn. The old Somerset stone building in which I had spent so many happy hours as a boy. What secrets was it harbouring? Perhaps it was the barn that Carl was interested in when he bought the field from old Weaver.

The Sherlock Holmes in me took over and I found myself trudging towards the building. The branch of an elderberry tree had penetrated one of the walls and protruded through the broken slates of the roof. The door was supposed to be secured with a large padlock, probably fixed by the police after their investigations, but time had eaten away at two panels. Entry was effected on hands and knees and fortunately, the sun was piercing the broken roof to give sufficient light.

I gulped as I realised that the police had not reinstated the excavations but the smell permeating the air was that of age and not humanity. My interest however, was not on the ground floor, which in my day was covered in cow dung. There was a hay loft, accessed by stone steps against a wall. Several of the lower ones were broken and I had difficulty pulling myself onto the loft.

In the old days, the loft held hay rakes and other tools but the only items remaining were some dusty boxes. My original determination was waning but instinct told me to prise open one, then all of them. I couldn't believe my eyes. Reels of cable, time switches, soldering equipment, and fuses. My excitement made me lose control of discretion. I was convinced that I was staring at the horde of stolen equipment from the wartime decoy. The villagers had been correct in their condemnation of the spy. The police must be informed.

I decided to drive to the village police station, but got no further than Hamm Cottage. There are times when it pays to listen to the inner voice and this was one of those occasions. I approached the cottage gate, through which I could see the lady seated in a deckchair on what used to be the lawn. I called out.

"Hello, may I talk to you? I've been poking around in your husband's barn."

"My ex-husband," she interrupted, "I divorced him when he went inside. Do what you like in the barn, but don't fall into the graves. I'm lucky it wasn't me in there."

There was a stunned silence brought on by her frankness. She was obviously embarrassed or defensive because she gazed into the distance, avoiding any eye contact. I tried to clear the air.

"This is our third meeting and I don't know your name. All I know is what the farmer told me."

"He knows nothing. It was the tittle-tattle in the village that broke up our marriage."

My doubts and suspicions turned to amazement as Jenny, as she introduced herself, unfolded an unbelievable tale. It was a story that began when she met Carl two months before they moved to Hamm Cottage. He had inherited the property from his uncle, also named Carl Langer, being the only surviving relative. When I queried this coincidence, Jenny hesitated before declaring that the uncle had been shot as a spy for disclosing secrets during the war via his family in Germany. The irony of it was that, with the exception of her husband, the complete Langer family had been killed during the bomber raids on Hamburg.

"Carl was happy here, at first and wanted to carry on with his hobby of inventing electrical gadgets. That's why he bought the barn. But things didn't go right and he became aggressive. He blamed me for being English and took advantage of my disability by confining me to the house and he started drinking heavily. Then came the village episode."

There was a need for me to say something.

"What is your disability?"

"I'm blind"

I stayed in the area for two weeks. At first, I continued to use my tent, but after several enjoyable outings with my new-found companion, I found myself head-over-heels in love.

"I want you to be my eyes," she whispered, "I want to enjoy your voice adding to the pictures that I have already painted in my mind of the lovely walks around here, or anywhere in the world."

THE CARNAGE THAT WAS CULLODEN

"Having seen all that I've seen and done all that I've done, I thought by now, I would be immune from all such emotion." This would have to be a really bloodthirsty tale.

The possibilities were endless. No, I didn't want another war story and the thought of a family disaster was unattractive. The answer came on the television when there was a rendering of The Battle of Culloden. I recalled seeing the actual fields where the Jacobites tried to re-instate the Stuarts back onto the Scottish and English thrones.

At the time of my visit I thought, "What a stupid place to choose to fight a battle; a boggy ground open to the elements and in a hostile area." My research confirmed my doubts and I tried to recapture the feelings of a local crofter caught up in the carnage.

THE CARNAGE THAT WAS CULLODEN

"Having seen all I've seen and done all I've done, I thought by now I would be immune to all such emotion, but ..." Twelve hours ago, those words were born in my torn mind. Six hours later they were re-born, prefaced by "My God, surely this cannot be so." Now, hiding in a small copse of pine trees bordering that bloody moor, I do not think I shall ever trust my eyes, or ears again.

Life had always been a struggle in the Highlands. My mother tried her best to maintain the smallholding after my father had gallantly paid the price of two arms, defending the clan's name against the marauding English bastards. At the age of eight I had been forced to witness the severing, as four drunken supporters of their monarch screamed abuse of the Maclachlan name. I had been left for dead with a deep cut across my chest. Fifteen years of sworn revenge had modelled my adult life.

My father ensured that from an early age, I would be taken regularly to a nearby clansman, Gerald for lessons in the use of his own firearm, dirk and broadsword.

"Listen, laddie, your own life will depend on your ability to adapt to the conditions of each battle field. If you are charging the enemy lines, it will be of no use relying on the firearm. After emptying the firearm chamber, throw it aside and grasp the broadsword. The dirk will be handy for cutting throats at close quarters."

Back at home, I practised with animal skins hanging on a line in the yard. Then came the call to support the Jacobite Rising, aimed at restoring the Stuarts to the Scottish and English thrones. A similar band had been formed in 1715, twenty nine years earlier but had been unsuccessful.

"This time will be different," Gerald boasted, "the French are joining in and are already landing on the West coast."

"Will Prince Charles Edward or Lord George Murray be our leader?"

"We're meeting up with Murray at Perth where we'll get our orders."

Three weeks later we had a skirmish at Edinburgh and then a nasty encounter at Prestonpans which I shall never forget. It was there that I killed my first man. The shame of what I had done hit me and I froze, staring at the pleading eyes of my prey. But I was instantly jerked back into the reality of the situation by Gerald, fighting alongside me.

"Well done laddie, now go for the second."

The third, fourth and fifth followed at Carlisle and we were on our way to London to claim the throne. But tiredness began to take its toll and at Derby, Lord Murray decided that with the non-appearance of the French and the increasing desertion, he should return to Scotland. It was fortunate for Prince Charles that we were all at hand for two long battles with the government forces commanded by the Duke of Cumberland at Falkirk and Stirling Castle.

But although we won both affairs, we learned to our dismay from two captured prisoners, that the Duke was planning a training camp at Aberdeen where he could muster a force of 9000 men, twice the size of we Scots. It was only the thought of my father that prevented me from returning home.

Gerald was convinced that it was our strategy of charging the enemy lines that frightened the opposition into submission. It was exciting to be part of it especially as our clan usually formed the extreme right flank in any charge, having the MacIntosh clan to our left. The combined noise as we went forward was inspiring. Living in the Highlands gave us the added advantage of being able to cope with the wet ground conditions.

Word came that Cumberland had crossed the Spey heading for Nairn and Charles sent hundreds of us to carry out a surprise night raid on their camp. It did not work, however, because they had a tip-off and I ran back with the rest to the main force which was now at Culloden.

There was an air of tension and disbelief in the camp and the mumbling in the tents reflected the discontent.

" Surely these boggy moors couldn't possibly be the spot that Lord Murray would choose for the biggest showdown."

"It's that Charles who's getting too cockey. He thinks we can win anywhere. He must be mad. How does he expect us to charge through that bog? We'll be mown down by their new 6-pounders."

"Not only that! There is no food in the camp and I've had just one small biscuit all day. Come on, let's go to the village and find food. No food, no fight, that's what I say."

I watched as dozens of my mates left the field while the clan leaders huddled in the comparative comfort of a sheltered copse, drinking the local brew. The night got colder and the April rain turned to sleet, dispelling any chance of the mutineers returning to camp. Our numbers were dwindling by the hour.

Morning brought rumours that Lord Murray had begged the Prince to change the choice of site for the impending battle, to no avail. The Prince was adamant, saying that he expected Cumberland to attack first, enabling the Highlanders to pick them off in the soft ground. By mid morning, I could see Lord Murray wandering amongst his men, stirring their spirits to give of their best that day. Suddenly, there was an exchange of fire convincing the Prince that he should withdraw to a safer place out of range of the artillery. That was the last I saw of him. He left without giving the anticipated order to charge. The weather chose this moment to add to our woes, and the cold wind which was blowing directly into our faces, brought sleet.

With nervous movements to and fro behind the two lines of Highlanders, Lord Murray could wait no longer for the Prince's order and bellowed out for the charge to begin. I had never seen so many men in a front line charge at the same time.

I was in the second line waiting for the order to follow. I could see that something had gone wrong. A bog on the left had restricted the width of the line, forcing the mass of screaming Highlanders to squeeze to the right. The right flank had nowhere to go, hemmed in by two dykes, beyond which riflemen of the fusiliers waited patiently. There was an uncanny silence at the far end of the field. The English had learned from previous encounters and were holding their fire until we had got to the point of no return.

Suddenly the Spring afternoon was shaken by the crescendo of hundreds of rifle shots firing simultaneously with the short 6-

pounders. The entire line of Highlanders in front of me was felled, as if blown over in a strong wind. "My God, surely this cannot be so," I thought. Amidst the smoke and screaming, the order for us to charge was given and the temporary reluctance to run to meet death reflected the shock shared by us all. But there was a lull in the firing. Time was needed by the fusiliers to reload. We rushed forward and our colleagues who had fallen in the first wave provided us with a cushion, giving our feet the luxury of not having to wade through boggy ground, enabling us to get close to the defences before they could fire a shot.

The fortune did not last long enough, and in the opening salvos, Gerald went down just ahead of me. Instinctively, I threw myself down by his side.

"They've got my legs," he cried, "leave me. You'll have to get my share of the bastards."

The anguish on his face made me look towards where his boots used to be. "If I leave you it'll be to go and get help for you. I lifted his head and thrust my water flask into his quivering mouth. I could see the resemblance of a smile. He grasped my hand. He wanted to talk about his home. Then he fainted in my arms.

I looked around me for help. The smoke was subsiding and except for the crying and groaning colleagues there was little movement. The firing had stopped and ahead at the place that had been my target, there was an eerie silence, followed by a roll on the drums and loud cheers. I had survived the battle.

Without knowing what I was doing I rushed back towards our original lines, searching for someone to help Gerald. There was nobody. The Highlanders were either lying on the battlefield or had run away. The government forces were leaving their positions having won the day. I ran in the opposite direction to the village where I hoped to find a bed for Gerald and help to carry him there. But to my dismay, the locals were not supportive of our cause and their aggression forced me to leave empty handed.

I returned to the moor, not knowing what to expect. But, as I got closer I realised that about forty fusiliers were returning to the battlefield. I hid in a small pine copse bordering the field. To my horror, I witnessed the most horrific aftermath of a battle. With accompanying shouts of "point, thrust and withdraw", the animals were walking amongst the fallen Highlanders, bayoneting any that moved. I stood helpless and sick.

"My God, surely this cannot be so. I shall never trust my eyes or ears again"

My mobile played "Amazing Grace" on the bagpipes. A text from dad. "Are you coming home for tea? Haven't you had enough War Games for today?"

FORGOTTEN HELL

Walter de la Mere wrote a superb poem "The Listeners". If you have never read it, these are the opening lines :-

" 'Is there anybody there?' said the traveller,
 Knocking on the moonlit door;
 And his horse in the silence champed the grasses
 Of the forest's ferny floor;
 And a bird flew up out of the turret,
 Above the traveller's head:
 And he smote upon the door again a second time;
 'Is there anybody there?' he said."

Eventually the traveller departs calling out that he had kept his word by returning. But it appears that the only live occupant was unable to speak.

My project sought to update the story behind the poem. My offering is a reminder of the suffering that was endured by our army fighting in Burma during the Second World War against the Japanese. In the jungle they were combating an unseen enemy, notorious for its barbaric and ruthless slaughter of prisoners. Our brave men were called the forgotten army and lived a forgotten hell.

FORGOTTEN HELL

There was a sudden crack as a twig snapped. Woody was right. Definitely, there was somebody ahead. Sgt. Platt's steadying hand on his arm was unnecessary. Both had stopped in their tracks, knowing only too well that, if they were caught by the Japs, it would mean certain death. They cowered in the tall undergrowth, frightened to breathe, scared to move. An eternity passed. Rivulets of sweat meandered gently around Woody's unblinking eyes, hesitated, and continued along a series of detours through his stubbled cheeks, blackened yesterday with the grease from his face powder compact, arriving at the corners of his mouth. He granted himself the pleasure of licking the moisture, ignoring the tickling sensations of the sweat elsewhere on his skin. Silence returned.

Perhaps an animal had caused the noise. This was the habitat of millions of tiny and not so tiny beasts, placed here on the edge of dense jungle, by nature, all of whom had their own predators and prey. None however was aware of the danger that either Woody or Platt was experiencing. Whilst Woody was a sprog in these conditions, Sgt. Platt's two years of jungle warfare had taught him the difference between a prancing monkey and a prying Jap sniper. No, this was for real. Dog eats dog. Kill or be killed. No thoughts of a poor suffering mother or wife bemoaning the tragic loss of loved ones. No rules apply. The law of the jungle had no greater meaning than this theatre of war. This was no ordinary conflict. No softening up by an air strike and ground artillery, followed by an advance protected by numerous tanks. No. This one-to-one combat demanded guile to outwit the cunning of the opposition. "Softly softly catchy monkey" was another unfortunate saying that belied the use of animal noises to confuse the enemy.

There was no wind that night. A full moon, however, was unhelpful, casting deceptive shadows amongst the jungle foliage. The brightness gave an eerie silvery effect to the stinking stagnant water and surrounding undergrowth. Their temporary refuge was adjacent to one of the many jungle pools in the swampy areas near Kabaw, 50 miles east of the Irrawaddy river. The silvery hue beautified all the trees and fauna in the open, whilst the shadowy areas were the hiding places for things of evil. Woody and Platt had to believe that every bush, every tree, every indentation in the landscape contained a message of unwelcome news, in the form of a suicidal Jap, willing to fight and die for his omnipotent Emperor Hirohita.

Woody began to imagine that his heart beats could be heard half a mile away. His chest pounded a beat that vibrated throughout his body uncontrollably. He wanted to tell the sergeant that he couldn't do anything about it, but Platt was too concerned with the control of his own feelings. Woody was convinced , in the same way that all the platoon soldiers were convinced, that Platt had no feelings. Not for those around him. Neither, probably, for any family at home and certainly not for himself. That's what made Sgt. Platt such a good soldier in this environment. That is why Lieutenant Geoffrey put him on this mission, a mission that must not fail.

They were all part of the forgotten army, the Chindits. Whilst the conventional armies nearer home were enjoying successes, the 14th army in Burma scarcely had any mention in the home press. The Australian Commander, General Bill Slim and the American General "Vinegar Joe" Stilwell had enjoyed great victories during early 1944, but supply lines became stretched and when 100,000 Japs made their assault, aimed at the eventual invasion of India, the Allies crumbled. The Japs, in turn suffered the same supply problem and Bill Slim was able to stop the advance just short of the Chin Hills, south of Imphal. Lieutenant Geoffrey was playing a role in restraining the southern flank and from their high ground, they had been able to radio vital information to HQ. Unfortunately a stray shell had killed the entire radio crew and destroyed their equipment, leaving the battalion with no means of communication with anybody. The assumption at HQ would be, that the entire battalion had been overrun. The lieutenant decided therefore, that, in the absence of any mechanisation in this part of the jungle and in spite of the possibility of encountering Jap patrols en route, two men should tackle the thirty miles on foot to enlighten the HQ staff of their plight and obtain replacement radio gear.

Woody's qualification for being selected for this dangerous mission was that he was of little use at base, being one of five ENSA (Entertainment National Service Association was a wartime organisation that provided entertainment for the troops fighting abroad) entertainers who had been in the wrong place at the wrong time, raising the moral of the Company just as the Japs began their assault. Consequently, they had been evacuated with the retreating troops. Woody's regret was that he lost his props consisting of a wind-up gramophone and old vinyl records which were the basis of his hilarious miming act.

But this was no time for airing his sense of humour. He was scared and fingered the bulging pocket of his tunic reassuring himself that the glass sphere containing the deadly vial of hazardous liquid was available if, God forbid, a Jap captured him without killing him. Since his arrival in Burma, he had been appalled at the atrocious manner by which allied servicemen had suffered at the hands of the Japs and he had no wish to add to their sadistic satisfaction.

Suddenly, the silence was broken by a series of squawks as the treetop inhabitants were rudely disturbed from their slumber. It was as if a Neighbourhood Watch, a future weapon against home intruders had been formed prematurely here in the jungle as a protection society. But the noise was sufficient to enable Platt and Woody to communicate quietly.

"They're there alright," whispered Platt. "Just wait till they show."

Woody gave a thumbs up and, half kneeling and half standing, he scanned the area over the silvery pool. He fingered the trigger of his rifle. The hurried training given to him at the time he volunteered to join the group of entertainers, did nothing to allay his fears of firing a gun. He could never overcome the anticipated kick-back that hurt his shoulder when the bullet was discharged and he couldn't get the hang of taking the first pressure of the trigger. Eyeing the pool glittering in the moonlight, he found himself recalling the beautiful picture drawn in his childhood autograph book by his famous art teacher, using only a quill pen, depicting a lad gazing through sunbeams trying to grasp castles in the sky. The thoughts gave him a longing to be anywhere but here.

The air was suddenly torn apart by a flash and a shot. Woody had turned, lowering his rifle in disbelief. Platt turned instinctively, just in time to see a dark shape hurtling into the pool.

"What the bloody ......"

Woody was shaking with uncontrollable fear. "I saw a movement reflected in the pool and ...."

"I don't believe it, you mean you just fired at a shadow!" Platt scoured the surrounding trees for another movement, but saw none. Recovering his composure, Woody checked his rifle and crouched lower, dreading the possible reaction of the Sgt.

"Well, that's settled that bastard's destiny. We'll mark our map calling that water "The Pool of Destiny". It's all quiet, so let's get out of here. I don't want to be around here if those nips get wind of our whereabouts, especially as I'm saddled with a comedian for company." Woody took that as a compliment. But what if he had missed.

Platt took up the lead and they made their way slowly and relentlessly through waist high undergrowth. By the time that Platt signalled the next stop, daylight was replacing the repressive darkness. For the first time since they had left the relative security of the battalion's position, Platt involved Woody in planning the route, with the aid of their guide, a rough map of the area, hastily drawn by the lieutenant on the only piece of paper that he could find in a hurry, torn from a pad of draft Death Certificates used by the admin officer when men had been killed. Pointing to a circle on the map, Platt indicated the possible location of the Company HQ.

"We must get there by tomorrow night."

They checked their remaining rations and agreed to restrict themselves to two meals, one in three hours time and the second early the next day. The Sgt. said that this would give them the incentive to keep going. Neither relished the thought of starving in this hell. The day that had started badly, gradually deteriorated. The humidity became unbearable and for an hour they traversed through ankle deep squelching mud, following what seemed to be an ancient path, partially disguised by overhanging foliage with razor sharp leaves, but going in the general direction of their destination.

"Shit!"

Platt let go of the expletive with venom. As Woody arrived at his side he realised the justification of the cry. The so-called path had brought them to a dead end, on the edge of a ravine. Ahead was a magnificent view but they had been following a road to nowhere. Now, they had to decide whether to go left or right.

"Sarg, it's late afternoon. If you think about it, with that rainbow over there, surely the sun is behind us. So we need to go left if we want to continue going north. If we go the other way, we might run into Japs."

Not wanting to take the words of a joker at face value, Platt consulted his map. Their only hope was that they had strayed off course and had come to the River Manipur. So perhaps laughing boy was right, after all. The decision was made, they went left and made good progress for about an hour, in spite of the rain. Suddenly they saw a stone building ahead. Instinctively, they both dived for cover, giving themselves the opportunity to think.

"If we were in Kent," whispered Platt, "I'd say it was a roadside inn. I wonder if they have Boddingtons."

"More like the shape of a church without any gravestones," replied Woody.

"OK clever bugger, you've been voted to go and investigate. Say your prayers and make a detour round to the other side. Report back before you go in."

Woody became smug. He certainly had made a contribution to their journey and here was another chance. His reconnoitre showed that there were two doors but no windows. His confidence began to get the better of him and he felt the need to check the doors before reporting back to the Sgt.

"Halt". Two men jumped him from behind and pinned him to the ground. "Name and number."

"2428022 Woody Woodbine, ENSA."

"Bloody funny. Are you trying to kid on that you have a booking in this temple? There's only room for a dozen."

Sgt. Platt heard the challenge and realised that they were with the allies. He broke cover and joined the patrol. The red rose flash on the tunic indicated one of the Lancashire regiments and an exchange of details revealed that they were from HQ. The interior of the building was completely bare, save for a small dusty religious icon in a corner.

"Probably originated from Tailand and stolen by the Burmese during one of their forages in the third century," mused Woody.

"OK clever boy, put the kettle on if you can conjure up something useful."

Stifled laughter filled the room. "First bit of humour we've had round here for six months. Nothing to laugh at."

The corporal leading the patrol listened to Platt's objective of obtaining replacement radio gear and instructed his wireless operator to report to HQ and seek advice.

"Suggest that we hand over our gear to Sgt. Platt and that we return to base. We could be back by nightfall."

"And if they throw in a map of the area I'll try and get them a show on our next tour," quipped Woody.

Contrary to normal procedure, acceptance of the proposal was radioed back immediately and Platt was briefed on the working practices and handed a wet dog-eared copy of call signs.

"I hope you've taken all that info on board, cos you'll be our radio op when we get back. Might as well do something useful."

Having scanned the maps at length, Platt decided to take a more westerly route home to avoid the confrontation with isolated Japs. This would take longer, but, having procured the radio equipment, the last thing that must happen was to lose the gear.

Their progress became slow and treacherous in the more mountainous route. Although they were following makeshift paths used by the peasants for their animals, the rain turned the earth into a yellow slimy sea of mud, clinging to the already sodden boots. The pair decided to forego sleeping for two days. By that time, they made a pitiful sight, reminiscent of the pictures they had seen of the forced marches of prisoners captured by the Japs earlier in the war. But it was now vital that the pair should succeed.

As they drew near to their target area, they sensed that something was wrong. They had anticipated making contact with Sections at the rear of their positions, but as they approached the summit of a hill that would have given them a view of the semi jungle in which the battalion had established their defences, all was still. Tired and drained of a desire to contend with another night in such conditions alone, the pair crouched and considered the situation. The radio equipment was heavy and Woody welcomed the opportunity to unload his back. They were in familiar territory and Platt could see the muddy stream that would lead them towards home. Five hours at the most, even though it would end uphill.

With renewed incentive, the pair lengthened their stride, determined to complete their onerous task. Woody felt particularly proud, anticipating an unusual pat on the back from the Lieutenant and also, the few war-weary soldiers who had gone out of their way to make his unplanned stay more bearable. Perhaps "Lefty" would even give up his rations for the night, as he had jocularly promised on their departure.

"You can have my corned beef when you pull back the tent flap carrying a new radio," Lefty had called out as parting words.

Platt was silent for the majority of the journey, content with setting a good pace and constantly looking up, down, left and right. The nearer they got to their camp, the faster he seemed to go, with no offer of a rest period. He was focussed on bringing the relief to his unit. Suddenly, Platt stopped, signalling Woody to join him.

"Ok boy, you can have the glory of breaking the news to the unit. You've done well. I don't say that very often. Round this corner you will see the clearing. That's base. They'll be sending out the evening patrol about now, so get in there quick. I'll hold back and keep you covered, just in case anything is wrong. And leave the radio here. Give one of your owl impressions when all is clear."

Relieved to discard the ton-weight packing, Woody wasted no time trudging the last two hundred yards in the fading light. On the edge of the clearing his stomach went sick. The fear that had caught him just before he had killed the Jap on the outward journey,

returned. The silence was eerie. This couldn't be right. He approached the first tent.
Hell !

"Is there anybody there?" whispered Woody,
Looking at the moonlit flap.
And his mud-filled boots champed the grasses
Of the jungle's ferny floor.
And a bird flew out of the tent
Above poor Woody's head
And he shook the flap a second time
"Is there anybody there?" he said.
But no one condescended to see
A triumphant Woody return
Nobody looked outside
Seeing him perplexed and still.

But only a host of phantom listeners
Remained inside the tent
Ten lifeless, headless soldiers brave
To their maker sent.
As he crept from tent to tent in silence
Never the least stir made the listeners
Though every word he spake
Were deadened by the shadowness of the still place.

In the last tent, from the one man left awake,
Emitted a sound, no tongue the words to make.
Aye, he heard the departing howl
Rasping through the air, a calling owl.

WAITING FOR THE "OFF"

I was playing golf, badly, and needed to pull myself together. Points were slipping away and my team was under threat. Ahead of me was a huge chestnut tree, right in the middle of the fairway. It was a cold winter's day, so with no leaves, it was the shape of the tree that caught my attention. "The barren, leaf-less chestnuts stand elegant and tall."

As a fair weather golfer, I compared my anticipation of Spring to that chestnut tree and nature in general. The tension went from my golf and the following poem took shape.

The barren, leaf-less chestnuts stand elegant and tall
No rising sap, just waiting there for Nature's Wake-Up call.
Through Winter months they're buffeted by endless wind and rain
Their tight-lipped buds keep straining to burst with life again.
Exposed and open branches force birds to look elsewhere
For cover from the snow and cold, the bitter months to bear.
But Nature has the answer , some trees no leaves they shed,
The evergreens, like holly give food and warmth instead.
The daffs start growing early, before the frost has formed.
Then stop, to wait until the frozen soil has really warmed.
But when New Year is over, with gardens white with snow
Perhaps, for weeks it lingers before it starts to go.
Then as the thaw brings solace, the ground returns in style
We find the cheeky snowdrop has been there all the while.
A buzz of expectation begins to fill the air
Deceptive sunny days appear and seem to be less rare.
But woe betide the buds that split, or mating that's begun
Late frosts and winds soon spoil the risk and nips the erring fun.
Then suddenly one morning we wake with quite a fright,
We're sure the hedge is greener and the sky is shining bright
The chestnut buds are popping; the birds brought in the dawn,
Nature sent its email, "A new Spring now is born".

When I was a boy I was taught that poems had a specific format; they should contain rhyming verses, scan and have a constant meter. Consequently, I find it difficult to appreciate modern trends of having uneven lines of words with no apparent design. But in accepting that tastes change, I wondered what the above poem would look like if it had been written by a modern poet.

AWAITING THE WAKE-UP CALL

Leaf-less chestnuts
Barren but elegant.
Winter buffeting, birds unwelcome.
Evergreens,
Offer berries and shelter.
Early daffodils
Pretend to grow,
Stop, waiting the call.
January snow
Discover cheeky snowdrops with thaw.

Winter sunshine deceives
Buds threaten to pop
Birds go house-hunting
Premature.
Late frosts reverts.

Suddenly,
Lasting sunshine, warmer soil.
Cry goes out
"Wake up, wake up"
Time to mate.
Spring is here.

CATS

It is a well-known fact in our village that I am not a cat lover. I am not keen on dogs either, or squirrels or mice. It is remembered locally that for a time, we had two cats in an endeavour to contain the mice population in our country garden. A lady in our writers group was obsessed with having cats as main characters in her stories. This prompted me to return home one evening and try and compete with her. The following story is a "tongue-in-cheek" account of my own experiences with the feline fraternity.

CATS

"Why don't you get a cat?"

Sod it. That was the last thing I wanted to hear. I wanted a scientific solution, not a practical one. I needed something like the answer given by the "Help" key when I had lost the use of data on my computer recently. "Try System Restore." And what happened? At the press of a button, the printer and computer were back on speaking terms as if nothing had ever gone wrong.

Why couldn't life be just as simple? If someone as archaic as me could grasp "System Restore", where is the problem? OK. Perhaps it was not possible for my runner bean seeds to re-appear in the potting shed, but surely there must be a solution, short of getting a cat!

"Why don't you? The mice would leave your beans alone."

We both love home-grown veg, especially runner beans and Dol was just as upset as I was when we discovered that all fifty two beans had been extracted from the flower pots and devoured during the night. But all was not lost. I went to the shed to retrieve the packet with the remainder of the Scarlet Emperor seeds.

"I'll start again and use the red anti-vermin dusting powder. I'll show them who's boss." But God wasn't on my side. The tell-tale hole in the packet pre-warned me, and sure enough, the cupboard was bare.

"Darling, I don't like you getting upset." We were in bed enjoying the nuptials that follow the departure of the kids to university. "Why don't you get a cat?"

Suddenly, I was no longer on heat. The urge was waning and the warmth of our king size bed had become the testing ground of feminine intrigue.

"I saw Judy today at the farm. She asked if I knew anybody who wanted a kitten."

I hesitated, withdrawing my hand from its task of caressing Dol's forehead. My silence gave away any chance of winning.

"A kitten has turned up in the barn and Frank will get rid of it if a home is not found. Judy says that, being an outside cat, it would remain that way and won't want to come indoors."

Oh yes, I'd heard it all before. My dislike of the feline fraternity had stemmed from the scratches I suffered whilst playing with next door's cat when I was about ten years old. Mrs. West who owned the beast said that I deserved all I got and had no right to drop it out of the bedroom window. It wasn't fair, really, because I was only trying to discover why it was, that, when I dropped a piece of toast, the buttered side always fell face down, but a cat falling from a window landed on its feet. I didn't have the courage to tie a piece of toast to the cat to test the result.

In later years when the dislike had festered into hatred, I watched the antics of cats and their control over families who had given them homes. I recalled vividly some nonsense at a nearby village happy home where a stray tabby came between husband and wife. Eventually, when a holiday was cancelled because of the cat's illness, the husband gave the wife an ultimatum. Her choice stunned the neighbourhood and she openly admitted that she missed her husband. In another household, the wife was adamant that the cat was allergic to the husband and he ended up sleeping in the spare room to make way for the cat to sleep at the foot of the wife's bed.

"Darling why don't we give it a try? I promise you, that if it stops us from going out, then we'll get rid of it." I was on the edge and the warm hand on my knee and the ensuing kiss sealed the deal.

"Alright, as long as we call it Buggerlugs."

From that moment on I was outnumbered. The new addition was the offspring of a multitude of mix 'n match adulterous encounters, judging by its coat. The first day in our garden was marred by the animal's misfortune of getting caught covering a pile of excreta which it had deposited in the spot where the beans were scheduled to be planted. A clod of earth thrown in its direction established the basis of our relationship for weeks to come.

The second day was even more horrendous. Judy arrived from the farm carrying the brother of our interloper, saying that it seemed cruel to leave this poor little kitten on its own. If we didn't want it, Frank would drown it. What a cunning strategy! So, it then became three against one. A casual observation about the strange shape of the new boarder, revealed that all was not well. Sam, as it was christened, was blind in one eye, had cat flu and was plagued with lice. It was at this point that Dol opened an account at the vet and its contents have remained a trade secret.

An old tea chest turned on its side in the shed became their home and I had to fork out good money to pay somebody to insert a cat-flap in the door. A blanket in pristine condition ensured that the little darlings stayed warm. An extra pint of milk per day was added to the housekeeping bill, but I drew a line at the prospect of chocolate digestives. Farm cats hunt for their sustenance and these were going to be trained as such. Catch mice or go hungry.

The next couple of weeks were put aside for training, but I'm not sure who was being trained. Cats believe in God and that he or she is a special cat. This gave Buggerlugs and Sam the divine right to do the training. They would hide somewhere for long periods and Dol, getting worried, gave me the task of finding them. Gradually I became accustomed to looking in the correct places. Next door's fishpond was an early favourite; up trees, or amongst the gooseberry bushes were also popular, resulting in playful meows as I extricated my scratched arms from the bushes.

Kittens are renowned for their entertaining qualities. "Aren't they clever," called Dol as she watched Sam scale the rose arbour and jump two feet onto the bird table, taking a blue tit by surprise and inviting it to accompany him to the seclusion of the rockery. I discovered later that Dol just managed to clear up the blue and yellow feathers before I appeared. There are certain things in this world that don't mix. Oil and water; little boys and washing; kippers and custard are examples. Cats and birds, cats and mice, cats and dogs, cats and me are other pairs that don't see eye to eye. Cats are the lowest common denominator in all this bloodshed and therefore, in my opinion, must be the root cause.

But one day just before his first birthday, Sam decided to demonstrate his ability to woo the opposition by introducing his "piece de resistance". He chose a sunny day with Dol and I sitting in the garden, to launch his comedy show, using a mouse as his fall guy. Blindness in one eye made it difficult for him to be as agile as Buggerlugs but the disability was the cornerstone of his act. He arrived through the hedge carrying his accomplice in his mouth and gently placed it on the grass in front of him. Sam was obviously a caring cat because, sensing that the mouse's back was itching, he began scratching it with sufficient pressure to restrain the creature from escaping.

At this point, Sam introduced his juggling prowess and threw his assistant into the air and lay on his side, tapping the grass, his good eye searching the heavens. What followed was unbelievable. After his flight in space the mouse landed with a thump, brushed himself down and crawled smartly back in the direction of his master. When he was about three feet away, he was engulfed in the outstretched paw of Sam who welcomed his return with a loving lick. Both remained perfectly still for several minutes until Sam, who had been eyeing me cautiously, sprang into action and tossed his quarry high in the air. Again, the slick training of the pair ensured that the mouse recovered from his flight and walked straight back for more tender loving care.

This charade was repeated three times before the coup de grace occurred. Sam turned onto his back, held the mouse up by its tail and devoured it head first. As the tail disappeared, Dol let out a scream that frightened Sam who rushed to the pond to wash down his lunch.

"What a disgusting cat, don't let him come near me."

"I don't agree. What a fantastic display. We've got a money-maker here."

I imagined the villagers at the next fete crowding round to see this performing cat. If only I could train him properly. Even if that idea failed I could keep a few mice handy for when we had visitors and I could give them cabaret. What a clever cat.

But I had underestimated the wiles of the omnipotent Sam who quickly realised his potential. Oh yes, he responded to training. He introduced some refinements of his own and we became regular features at local fund raising events. But there was a cost involved. Dol, who had given me an ultimatum, is no longer my partner. She has been replaced and digestives are a permanent feature in the diet. Sam moved indoors of course and I have to sleep in the spare room. Nothing is sacred anymore. Even my computer mouse has teeth marks on it and there is a strange smell of tuna when I turn on the computer. And who is Fluffy, who keeps sending me emails?

LOVE MATCH

"A Love Lost, Found, and Lost Again".
The Chairman of the writers group beamed with enthusiasm as he specified the subject matter.
"Let you imagination run riot. You'll need about 2000 words to do justice to this."
The natural choice of dealing with this topic would be the elderly couple becoming an item again, thirty years after splitting up. But I wanted something different. Then I saw an Ad in the Lonely Hearts section of the County paper.
"Male Author, own country house ...." Why on earth would a man with his own property want a companion who also owned a house? It seemed fishy to me.

LOVE MATCH

"MALE AUTHOR, 60's, own country house, enjoys the major pleasures of life .. .... dining, wining and travel, seeks full of fun, non- smoking, home owning lady, with similar pursuits for lasting relationship."

"Yes!"

Kay snapped her fingers at the "Getting Together" advert.

"Yes, yes, yes."

She planted a decisive tick with her marking pen against the Box No.242. The previous entries, with one exception, had been stroked out of recognition unceremoniously. The one question mark highlighted an older man who appeared to be less pompous than the majority, but retained a certain "sans foix" to make him attractive.

Kay poured yet another black coffee from the cafetierre and eyed the telephone.

"No, this must be planned," she thought, searching through the pile of unread papers and magazines for her "aide-memoire" that listed all the questions demanding answers from a potential companion. She couldn't rely on her ultra-vague memory to clear the minefield of potentially stupid statements that may fall from her lips at their first contact.

For the umpteenth time Kay held a pretend conversation with her telephone handset. Suddenly, on impulse, she dialled the magazine and asked for the Box Number registry.

"You can either write to us enclosing a sealed letter for the Box Holder, or leave a contact telephone number with me and await a call. In all instances, you have the assurance of complete confidentiality within our organisation."

"So that's how it works," she replied, disclosing her home number and jotting down her safeguard reference.

Her coffee, though cold, calmed her and she lay back on her sofa-bed, mulling over the sequence of events that had subjected her to this embarrassing mode of living. Her single room flat above a Swanscombe fish and chip shop reflected the depths to which she had sunk. In her earlier days she had enjoyed the high-life of party-going with the upper set. Her husband was a crook and they had divorced after he had been sent down for ten years. Kay's heart got her involved with a compulsive gambler. However, when her beaux ditched her, he took, not only his own life, but all of her sizeable wealth, by means of extensive debts. She was lucky that the flat contained the telephone, which rang occasionally with an invitation, but her inability to return hospitality led to the offers becoming few and far between.

Len had suffered enough. The good times of the sixties were a distant memory. Those were the days when he and Hilary hit the jackpot with the football coupons and had rocketed-up the social scale. Their secluded detached five bedroom house on the North Downs was the envy of all who were lucky enough to be invited to their house parties. It was an ideal environment to carry on with his writing career. Hilary was an exciting lover; perhaps too exciting. It contributed to their downfall. While Len spent hours writing, Hilary began tasting the fruits on the other side of the fence. Within a few horrendous months, Len lost his wife, his house and his zest for living. Together with her new-found barrister lover, Hilary schemed a plot that had left him almost bankrupt and totally humiliated.

Condemned to a two-roomed squat in Rochester, Len hit the bottle, reneged on his writing contract and gradually sunk to his current state of despair. Petty burglaries had become his source of entertainment. The only friend who stayed with him was his car. He relied on the Toyota to give him perhaps his only contact with humanity: a casual short drive, usually to a pub.

It was on one such outing during a day of summer rain, sheltering in a hotel car park, rummaging amongst the glove compartment rubbish, that he discovered the key to his old house. He toyed with it for several minutes until the memories got the better of him and his Toyota friend responded by whisking him towards the property.

Len had no plans for dealing with any awkward questions and had no idea who he might meet. There were no cars to greet him so he drove up to the front door, alighted and circled the house. The rear entrance looked inviting and Len risked the bell twice. His luck held when he tried the key and doubly so when he found the alarm box key was still in situ, allowing him to bring silence to the place. He looked around the ground floor in awe. Dust sheets covered much of the furniture, there was no food in the kitchen and two clocks were the only ornaments.

On his homeward journey, Len imagined that Christmas had come early. The occupants were obviously on an extended foreign trip, leaving him with unbounded opportunities. By the time that he had consumed three large scotches, his world had turned rightside-up and he found himself drafting an advert for the Lonely Hearts Club magazine for a partner to share his good fortune.

Kay changed her plan of action several times during the three day wait for the phone to bring her the news that she so dearly longed to hear. A photo of her old home would suffice as evidence of her background. She hoped that by the time the suitor wanted to see it, her body should have won him over. Her confidence grew and as she replaced the receiver after speaking to the author, she congratulated herself for engineering their first date in two days' time, at a Maidstone pub. He had sounded confident, jolly and charming without being over-complimentary. He had a soft attractive voice which appealed to her and he certainly sounded enthusiastic.

Len wasted no time in restoring the kitchen, lounge and one bedroom of the new-found property, to a liveable state. It would be dark if the lady visited that week and in any case, a single man's pad would harbour dust, so there was no need to be too fussy.

The introductions at the Galloping Horse were tentative and painstaking, each dealing with a hurdle as it surfaced. Neither wished to be pushy and both had good reasons for not divulging too much too soon. Gradually, however, the tongues loosened and Len felt that progress was being made. Kay was already stirring his inner self.

"Yes, I'd love to see your home," she said. "You're obviously proud of it and yes, Eastbourne sounds exciting for next Tuesday. Great." Kay leant forward and patted his thigh, perhaps a little higher than she had intended. "I didn't expect a second date so early."

The challenge was in gear and Len guided her towards his Toyota. "We'll leave your car here and I'll bring you back."

The evening clouds were gathering as they climbed the country lanes to Len's house. As they approached the driveway, Kay gasped and tried to restrain an "Aaaah".

"Why are you so startled? You frightened me for a minute."

"I'm sorry, it's .... I ... it's not what I had expected."

Len led the way round the back and through the alarmed door. Peace was established. He went into the hall to illuminate the downstairs and returned to the kitchen.

"You wander about and I'll sort out some beers for us. Feel free to roam anywhere."

Kay did just that. She left her jacket and bag on the kitchen table and made for the lounge. Why had fate brought her back to the house that had been her home for all those happy years? Why should this man be entitled to enjoy her home? She retraced her steps into the hall only to see the reflections in the tall mirror, of Len in the kitchen picking the contents of her bag from the floor.

"Sorry about that," he called, as Kay burst in. "I caught it with my arm. Here's your beer. Do you like what you see?"

Kay decided to get a grip of herself. She needed time to think; time to plan.

"Yes, it's lovely. I'm glad I've seen it. You could get lost in it." Half of her beer disappeared in three gulps. "I think I'd better be making way home before it gets too dark."

She waited in the car while the confused Len locked up. Why the sudden need to go? Had he cocked it up with the handbag episode? They remained silent and Len stopped for petrol. Instinctively, as soon as she was alone Kay opened the glove compartment where she knew she would find the house key. She felt better; this would give her another option.

Len found a new Kay on his return. Her silence had been replaced with a bubbling enthusiasm, making suggestions for Eastbourne. On their arrival at the pub car park she kissed him willingly before leaving, but her only words were, "I'll await a call about your plans for Eastbourne."

As he turned onto the Rochester road, Len gave himself nought out of ten for the handbag routine but smiled at his achievement of noting her address on her driving license and her Visa credit card details. The big worry was, "Where did she find the picture of the house? She had only been left alone in the place for a minute or two. It must have been on the table when they entered."

By the time he had downed his second scotch, he had decided not to get tangled with Kay. Something was amiss. He was not in control and he didn't like it. He began to get cross and found himself planning ways of using the information that he had plundered.

Kay couldn't sleep. Memories of the house kept surfacing with thoughts of how her handbag had become unzipped. The resentment of her loss steered her towards a kind of revenge. The key would give her the ability to achieve a deal of satisfaction if she could hold her nerve. Her first port of call in the morning was the library. Len had talked a lot during their pub visit but had said little about himself. One item that had stuck in her mind however, was that he had written a book "A Love Lost, Found and Lost Again". The librarian steered Kay through the intricacies of using a computer and left her in the hands of Jeeves. To her astonishment she was faced immediately with a synopsis of the story by Leonard Ashton together with his picture taken when he was much younger.

Curiosity made her scan the story line. It concerned a jilted male chauvinist who set out to get revenge on the man who stole his dream but ended up in prison, losing everything else in addition to his lover. Kay copied the excerpt and sat in her car finalising her plan.

Len searched the High Street for number 7a. It didn't exist. He was expecting a semi, at least. Kay had the grandeur of better things than this. He abandoned his car and traced the numerical sequence on foot. The secret lay behind the fish shop where a fire escape staircase led to a flat. His knock was unanswered and within seconds he was inside. Kay's photos confirmed the legitimacy of his plans. With the exception of a £20 note and a few trinkets, which he pocketed, he could see nothing of value and he set to work trashing the place. His conviction that she intended to fleece him drove him to more destructive lengths.

Kay left her vehicle in a lay-by and walked purposefully up the drive to her old house. Thankfully, Len was not in and her key gained her entrance. With all the time in the world, she wandered from room to room marvelling at the sheer wealth of the man and eyeing several bits that she was sure he wouldn't miss. She could only assume that the dust covers in many of the rooms were the actions of a person living alone. She had intended to embark on a mission of theft but her growing anger at having lost her home to this undeserving man, fired her to greater devastation.

With her car now moved to the rear door, Kay systematically transferred to it items that attracted her. She felt calmer now. Everything was going to plan. The final acts were to turn on the electric fire close to the dust covers in the second lounge and put towels on the ignited cooker in the kitchen, set the alarm and lock up. On leaving the house she placed her photo of the house and the book excerpt at the garage entrance.

Kay was not prepared for the shock awaiting her in Swanscombe.

"Leonard Ashton? We would like to ask you a few questions about Downs House. May we come in?"

"We would also like to know your whereabouts yesterday. Your car was seen in the vicinity of the Swanscombe fish shop fire. We just want to eliminate you from that enquiry. One fire in a day is enough for anyone!"

FREE FROM FEAR

"Jocelyn Armby Liked To Be Frightened". This is another example of the writers group specifying the first line of a 1500 word story.

I think you will agree that this story almost got out of hand, bordering on fantasy. But, wait a minute. Three months after I had submitted the story to the group, I watched a television UK History programme documenting the antics of spies during and after the Second World War. How could I have had the premonition of a post-war exploit that hitherto had received no publicity?

FREE FROM FEAR

"JOCELYN ARMBY LIKED TO BE FRIGHTENED". It was there for all to see. Her headstone in the tiny chapel cemetery at Carbridge, near Inverness, Scotland summed up her life, although it is doubtful whether anyone except me understands the reason for the odd epitaph. So why had I been singled out to unravel the mystery ?

It was my own fault, I suppose. Whilst touring Scotland in 1988 a radio programme depicting amusing gravestone epitaphs forced me to re-arrange my schedule and find this place. Surely, Jocelyn would fit that old cliché, "Flying By The Seat Of Your Pants" and be the subject matter for my next short story. The report was confirmed. "Born September 1915 ... Died October 1987".

The chapel warden put me on the trail. Jocelyn had arrived in the village thirty years previously and had kept herself in a rented bungalow on the outskirts of Carbridge, having the minimum of contact with the locals. She had become a heroine overnight, however, when, at the age of sixty, she had dived from the village bridge to save two young children in the swollen river. The boys had persistently flouted warnings against the practice of playing "chicken" from the bridge, trying to dive as close as possible to the rocky banks. She played down the plaudits of the Council and parishioners at a civic recognition ceremony, saying that she had acted because of fear.

Jocelyn had confided in the warden that fear had dominated her life, saying that she performed better when scared. She had chosen the epitaph but would not elaborate on her story. Without any relatives, she had asked the warden to dispose of the contents of the bungalow on her demise, with the proceeds financing her burial in the village and any balance to be used for the benefit of villagers. Whilst on a visit to Kent, in England, Jocelyn had decided quite stupidly to venture outside during the hurricane which struck the South and was killed by a falling tree. The temptation to fight the elements had been her undoing and the warden was still carrying out her wishes at the time of my visit.

Gaining possession of the key for 24 hours was not a problem and I assured the warden that my motives were purely to acquire the background atmosphere for my story about Jocelyn.

Although most of the furniture had gone, files and bundles of papers were stacked tidily in one of the rooms. After three hours of glancing through the piles, it occurred to me that there were no photos of any family or friends and the papers were entirely of matters relating to her stay in Carbridge. What on earth had happened to her previous 40 years? Where had she lived as a child and why had she destroyed the mountain of keepsakes that we all hoard during a lifetime? Why did she have no pension, no passport, no bank statements or credit cards ? The warden confirmed the situation as I had seen it and added that even her car had been leased. More surprising was the realisation that Jocelyn always paid cash for debts. She had never called on a doctor or dentist in Carbridge.

I returned to the bungalow, confused and more determined. The challenge had gripped me, but I needed a breakthrough. It came on the discovery of a stick with a hook on it, leaning beside the bathroom door. I walked around the rooms, tapping my hand with the stick, searching for the link. It was on the ceiling of the bathroom ... a trap door into the loft. Pressure on the trap, with the stick, released the cover and a ladder was revealed. The hook made the ladder accessible and I was able to recommence the treasure hunt.

A rodent of sorts scurried away as I found the light switch, causing me to shiver, but the immediate sight of two cases took the creature from my mind. Surely, the key to the solution was at hand. The nearest case was close enough to the entrance for me to handle without having to climb into the loft. Although my heart was pounding with anticipation, I was not prepared for the shock that awaited me. The dusty lid was unlocked, but resisted my attempts to open it. A determined shake did the trick and I was faced with a real Aladdin's cave.

I froze. In front of me were sheafs of £20 notes.

I gripped the surrounds of the entrance and blinked. At first I was unable to touch the find, but as the shock diminished, I took one wad of notes and started counting. Twenty five £20 notes, £500. There were other piles of £50 notes. A rough assessment of the number of piles gave me a quick, startled estimate of £50,000.

For no apparent reason, I descended the ladder and sat on the floor. My thoughts went to the warden whose problems, surely must be over. But I was no nearer the breakthrough for my story. Entering the loft, I reached for the second, heavier case and lowered it to the ground to enable me to search in greater comfort. Unfortunately, it was locked and with the bungalow in its present state I decided immediately to retreat to my hotel with both cases, returning the key without comment to the warden's wife, saying that a further visit may be necessary.

Surgery was required to operate on the contents of the case and the five hours of sorting, reading, cross-checking and thinking took me into the early morning, by which time my brain hurt. An amazing story was unfolding, with sufficient written material to form the backbone of my story, without recourse to fiction.

Photos and reports told of a childhood in Kenya on a game reserve and this obviously prompted the desire to be frightened. Pictures showed Jocelyn in a tree with a leopard prowling below. The family came to England in 1938, but whilst Jocelyn was serving in the Army during the 2nd world war, all of her family were killed in an air raid on London. Devastated, she volunteered for a Special Operations Group where promotion ensured a life of danger. Parachuted into occupied France, there followed twelve months of unbelievable daring as she infiltrated the inner ring of the German "Gestapo", altering records of known French resistance workers, aiding the escape of sentenced heroes and on one outrageous occasion, posing as a doctor, she injected the Head of Gestapo at Lille with syphilis. She was withdrawn from France during an audacious pick-up on the French coast, in order to act for intelligence in Russia. It was there that several attempts on her life were staged, resulting in her hasty withdrawal.

The war had ended long before her most dangerous mission. All attempts to quell the Mafia who were bringing Italy to its knees, had failed and the advice of the UK Intelligence was sought. With the Russian hit men seeking to kill her, she turned up in Milan setting a trap for the Grandfather (or Godfather) of the leading family. Having left false clues incriminating the son of the rivals, she ambushed and killed the entire occupants of the car in which the Godfather was travelling, thereby sparking the removal by murder of the major opponents in the Mafia war. But rumours spread and our hero required desperate measures to survive.

It was at this point of foraging amongst the papers that I discovered that we had all been hoodwinked. Jocelyn was not a female at all. She, or rather, he, was born Jon Cley and called Barmy Jon Cley in the army. Now, with vultures on his trail, he chose the anagram Jocelyn Armby to be his new identity. His army records were destroyed and to this day, the Army deny all knowledge of either name, but Jocelyn came away with the equivalent of £400,000 in today's money in unmarked notes to tide him over the remaining years, never knowing whether the next visitor would be his undoing.

Standing this evening over her, I mean, his grave, I smiled. Fifteen years ago, I stood here, full of eager intention to write the most amazing story of the war. Somehow the urge disappeared when I lay in bed wondering what to do with the papers .... and money. I made the decision. I thanked the warden for his help, but said that there didn't seem to be a story after all. The papers? Well, after the efforts to conceal his identity, it wasn't my job to expose him. And the money? Investments in gold proved to be a wonderful recommendation and I have since enjoyed trips to Lille, St. Petersburg, Moscow, and Milan; all beautiful spots for a bit of intrigue.

THE HAUNTED HEAVEN

I am not a supporter of stories about ghosts, science fiction or fantasy. In fact, I am in a minority at the Writers Group, many members of which are extremely adept in that genre. Consequently, I did not relish the challenge to sink into the abyss and write my expectations of the "After-world".

I had to dig deep to get started, but it took 2,400 words for me to extricate myself from the mire of improbability.

THE HAUNTED HEAVEN

A single shot rang out and the echo reverberated around the enclosed courtyard of the apartment block. Instinctively, my eyes focussed on the second floor. For a moment in the gloom, I was certain that a hooded man ran from the direction of Jenny's door and disappeared down the central stairwell. I sprinted towards the building and climbed the stairs two at a time, desperate to dispel the fear that Jenny was in danger.

It was not to be. Through the open door, her groans were ominous and I rushed into the bedroom, the room that held so many thrilling memories. I found my lover writhing on the blood-splattered bed. I screamed and cradled her in my arms, begging her to open her eyes. She responded with a half smile, gasping for breath.

"Come .. with .. me," she whispered, "darling, come with me." And after a pained pause, "if only you had married me. Hold me ... I'm going darling ... I will haunt you till you join me."

Then it was over. I closed her eyelids and kissed her forehead for the last time. Emotion took over and I sank to the floor, still grasping her hand. I collapsed there and, for a while, cried uncontrollably. My mind darted from one "if only" ... to another. Could I have prevented her from leaving Alex her jealous husband? Should I have left my own family to begin again with her?

An hour later, the evening cold and darkness in the room brought me back to reality and survival became important. Assuming Alex had carried out this murder and had seen me downstairs, he could be waiting. Worse still ... suppose a neighbour had seen me and alerted the police. Suddenly I felt an urgent need to disappear. My head hurt with the guilt of leaving Jenny's body in a pool of blood just to save my own skin. But the realisation that I would be expected home from work coloured my thinking.

I set off for home, but with less than a third of my journey completed, I could go no further and drove into a wooded car park frequented by Jenny and me on many occasions. As I sat on a bench, pondering over the mess that I had created, I became conscious of company.

"Come with me darling." A hand moved from my knee to my own hand.

"Hold me."

A shiver raced from my spine to my toes. If this was Jenny, was I going mad? Had the shock started giving me hallucinations? The sound and feeling was too real to be a dream. I instinctively reached out to my left but there was nothing. She was still with me, I could tell and the sudden coldness that had accompanied the voice, remained with me.

"Keep me in your heart, I'll be waiting." I was alone once more and sat petrified for several minutes before recovering.

There was no escape. During the following weeks my family, friends and workmates pestered me with enquiries as to my unusually sullen moods. Whilst I had not fired the fatal shot, I still felt responsible for Jenny's death. Her departure had undoubtedly released me from the impossible burden of living two parallel lives of deceit, but since then I had found a new "me" and I didn't like what I saw.

I cannot be the first man to say that I had not intended to get entangled with another woman. I was happy enough at home and led a busy work and social life. But in a moment of bravado I had chosen to interpret a glance from a complete stranger at a party as an invitation to flirt and things progressed from there. A visit for coffee led to more purposeful assignations and then I was hooked. Jenny was a temptress and at times of frenzied activity she pressed for a more permanent relationship. Her contention that she had been searching for a special kind of lover to take into the next world added to my sense of pride and I couldn't let go.

As the relationship developed, her predictions about the manner of our continued partnership in the after-world became more emphatic. On several occasions, as we lay recounting the pleasure of the previous hours, I felt that although she was in my arms, her mind was elsewhere. Whilst I was sure that I was her only physical pastime, her deep expectations of life after death, planted seeds of caution in my mind. My use of the church had been restricted to visits of convenience and consequently I had never considered the possibility of the world envisaged by Jenny. Her words were uncanny. She did not refer to religion but her continued reference to minute details of a location, gave me a fear of prolonging conversations on this topic. Her favourite expression when I refused to comment was, "Come with me. I will haunt you until you do." And we would laugh.

I remembered the day when she told me that she had left her husband.

"I will find a place to live until you join me."

I tried to keep a low profile, fearing the possibility of being exposed as the cause of the breakdown of their marriage. As a hard businessman and being aggressive at home, Alex was not an opponent with whom I would relish a confrontation. Gradually, however, our ventures got back on track and Jenny's new apartment home became the venue for venting our passion.

But now I had to live with this vision of her death. Nightmares occurred continually. Jenny's blood poured over me. I was hounded by animals with Alex's features. When I tried to grasp her, my hands passed through her transparent body. For two weeks this recurring dream continued unabated, until it was replaced by a terrifying series of searching examinations of my whole being.

Each night became more tortuous and after fighting the urge to sleep I was chased, terrified through torrents of water by a herd of animals. As I was driven towards a dome-like structure, the building changed its shape to resemble the herd. I ran up the steep yellow winding path to its summit with the animals snapping at my heels. There I became trapped. With the baying pursuers shaking the foundation of the prison, I was subjected to an in-depth scrutiny of my behaviour.

On the first night, my belief in God was challenged and I was charged with having more than one God or devil to suit my desire. At the slightest hint that I was deviating from the truth, my body spun round the structure with the threat of being thrown to the animals. The interrogator knew of my shortcomings and punished me for any attempt to lie. When my words were eventually believed, a soft, gentle, feminine voice comforted me and I was allowed to wake from my sleep.

The second night became a desperate race with saliva-dribbling wolves, eager to tear me apart. But as I approached the dome, the structure took on the frightening appearance of a wolf ripping a large animal to pieces. In spite of the fear within me and with a superhuman effort I managed to gain the entrance of the refuge, just as the leading predator tore at my leg. The reception inside gave me no respite and I had to find words to defend my continual abuse of the Sabbath and the use of the Lord's name to justify my wrong-doings. This time water almost filled the dome and as my unsatisfactory answers were punished, I experienced the fear that my lungs might explode with my inability to breathe. On this occasion I awoke and found myself sitting bolt upright in bed with sweat pouring from me.

I always suffered from the fear of snakes and the third night brought this terror to the brink. Not only were the reptiles fast and large but the long wavy structure chosen for the character testing, had brightly coloured specimens hanging precariously from the roof, flicking their fangs dangerously close to my face. The subject for that evening related to my indifference to my parents and my attitude to killing God's creatures. The angel voice readily noted that my indiscriminate killings had been restricted to vermin and I was given a token brush with the vipers to remind me that the misdemeanour was not acceptable. But my failures regarding my mother and father, in the opinion of the aggressive interviewer were atrocious and I found myself screaming in the pit of adult snakes inciting their young to slither up and down my body.

Things were getting serious at home. My irritability led to arguments and for two nights I refused to go to bed. I walked the streets rather than subject myself to the trauma of sleeping. Sensing that I was close to a breakdown, my wife sent for a doctor. I succumbed to swallowing two tablets, thinking quite stupidly that enforced drugged sleep would, somehow, be different. If anything, the outcome proved to be worse and birds, thousands of them, chased me relentlessly. I splashed through water up to my waist in an effort to protect myself but the pecking at my head left me screaming for help.

My wife woke me, but only for the minute that allowed me to wipe the sweat from my brow, before resuming the sleep. The dome was now a birdhouse and the penal topics were my stealing tendencies as a boy and my adulterous behaviour as a man. My efforts to excuse my inability to overcome the need to steal, surprisingly was accepted by the voice which then seemed to want to concentrate on my record since my marriage. I tried in vain to say that I wasn't the guilty party on each of the occasions when I wandered and there was a sudden rush of air as hundreds of birds lifted me up and twisted me around the dome at speed, allowing me to crash against the sides. Each time the flurry stopped, the voice probed deeper, prompting me to analyse the reasons for my actions and the pleasure that I may have brought upon the recipients. As the punishment subsided, I gained the startling impression that to commit adultery was right and proper. My return to pleasant slumber was sudden and welcome.

For the whole of the following day my brain was awash with the meaning of my nightly torment. Without reaching any conclusion I went to sleep, actually wanting to see what the night had in store. But the immediate involvement was as vicious as on any previous evening. Vermin in their hundreds jumped at me, scratching me with their tiny claws and jumping at me from overhanging branches. I had never seen so many squirrels, all anxious to attack my face. The chase was frightening and seemed never-ending. From inside the dome, which had now taken the shape of the rat-like creatures, a voice lifted me to its safety. The interview topic of the night referred to my envy; the envy of my neighbours' possessions, including their wives and the attraction of giving false evidence against the neighbours. I suddenly grasped the opportunity to challenge my tormentor and said that I saw no wrong in enjoying the company of my neighbour's wife. The voice showed interest in my assertion.

"If the wife was attractive enough for you to forsake all else to acquire the lady, then an approach to her could be condoned, but not as a plaything." I remained silent, awaiting a further explanation.

"Did you know of anyone in your philandering, with whom you could enjoy permanent pleasure?" I did not reply.

The irony of the situation was that, while the nightmares ceased at that point, sleepless nights followed. The interrogations had lost their meanings and I completely overlooked the change of emphasis for deciding right from wrong as depicted on the final night.

Several days later I got the sudden urge to return to the wooded park that I had visited on the night of Jenny's death. As I approached the same seat as before, Jenny appeared beside me, grasping my hands and raining kisses on my cheeks. I could smell her favourite perfume and her whispers were as intoxicating as they always had been when we made love. Unlike the previous visitation in the park, this time Jenny had substance and I could feel the soft texture of her skin.

"Why are you torturing me Jenny?"

"You are torturing yourself. You always wanted to join me but lacked the courage. Come with me. Our place is prepared."

Jenny disappeared.

Depression took over and my life started to disintegrate. I tried to recall the causes of our relationship and the unhappiness that Jenny had suffered in her own marriage. I wanted to blame Alex. In a desperate attempt to rid myself of this darkness, I made a foolhardy decision and went to confront him.

A single shot rang out. This time it was in my head that the echo reverberated. I felt no pain, but was conscious of being lifted and spiralled through space, accompanied by a choir of harmonising angels. A feeling of being thrust through turbulent clouds accentuated the uncontrollable state of my earthly being. But gone was the urge to seek remedies to counteract my condition. Gradually, the dizziness subsided, the singing softened into a gentle humming and the movement tempered into a floating sensation inspired by a silent zephyr. There was no magic carpet to hold my weightless body. No wings to perpetuate my gliding. There was no feeling of movement at all.

"I knew you would come and I am pleased."

Dressed in a beautifully embroidered silk kaftan, Jenny had appeared beside me and cradled me in her arms. With a stance resembling a loving couple fox-trotting across a ballroom floor, we danced through the universe. Suddenly, I noticed a familiar sight, that of a spiralling yellow path leading upwards to a dome. But the structure that had housed so many dark memories for me, had been transformed into a shape resembling four shining bells, each tolling a welcome for us.

"When I returned to earth to seek a partner I could never have anticipated finding a more loving person. You have proved to me that you are the man who must accompany me to my special home in the heavens. The inquisition that you endured enables us to by-pass the spiral dome and drift upwards to that silvery palace in the distance. Come Darling."

160

HONOUR RESTORED

A local pub has a treasured photograph of the Australian Services XI cricket team that played several Test Matches against England immediately after the Second World War. I remember watching the Lords Test instead of going to school.

I could not put a name to one of the officials in the photograph and my imagination led me to suppose that he was the publican displaying the photo. The following story could be the answer.

HONOUR RESTORED

"Hey, Jenny, come over here and dig this!"
Jenny dutifully placed her gin and orange on the brightly polished table, scraped her chair noisily on the stone floor and reluctantly left the comparative warmth of the smoky imitation of a fire. Charlotte, the smiling landlady of The Brigadier Gerard, had already explained on their arrival that the coal ration was not due to be delivered until the following week and that the wooden blocks that they were trying to burn were damp and unfriendly. It was the smoke and not the heat that wafted with her across the Tap Room to where Brian was studying a series of photos surrounding an autographed cricket bat mounted on the wall.

"Would you believe it? The Australian Services XI v Kent XI Horton Regis, Saturday, July 14th 1945, only two years ago."

Her husband fingered the pictures admiringly.

"Look, Lindsay Hassett, he became Australian captain in 1946, Keith Miller, Stan Sismey, and Graham Williams. I thought he was a prisoner of war in Germany. He must have just got out."

"I expect Roger would have known most of them," sighed Jenny.

A shiver went through her body as her words acted as a reminder of their mission in England. Back home in Sydney, their only son Roger had answered a call for volunteers to join the Australian forces to help Britain. In 1940 he had been sent to England to train as fighter pilot. Within five weeks he was posted to RAF Biggin Hill where he joined a squadron of RAAF Spitfires. He was the last pilot to be killed in the Battle of Britain. His resting place was in the churchyard of All Saints, Horton Regis. She was not certain that she wanted to see her nineteen year old son's grave but when the opportunity came for Brian to attend a conference in London, she jumped at the chance. Now, however, she didn't want tomorrow to come.

"But who can that be? He's in all the pictures but I can't place him. I recognise the face, especially the nose, but that's all. Who on earth …"

"That's the landlord, Keith." The only other occupants of the bar, two elderly men, had joined them at the cricket mementos.

"What a weekend! I'd say that was the best match that these parts have ever seen. All the Aussie servicemen who were playing in the Victory Tests and half the England side led by Kent's keeper Les Ames turned up. They lost three balls with the close boundaries and big hitting!"

"He brought them here, did Keith. Seemed to know 'em all. Mind you, he made a few bob in the bar after the match."

The door of the private room opened and landlord Keith joined his pretty wife behind the bar.

"Better leave the fire alone. It may last the evening. Who have we here? Interested in cricket are you?"

"Not really," said Brian, focussing his gaze on the nose, "more interested in people. We're over from Sydney to see our son's grave, Roger Fingleton of the RAAF.

Jenny gazed forlornly at the November afternoon sky. Sydney's coathanger bridge was silhouetted against a backcloth of threatening white balloons of clouds. The trams, for which the bridge was built four years earlier in 1932, could be seen quite clearly, a sign which forecast rain.

"Could be wet tonight." Brian joined her at the bay window overlooking the estuary. Before he could reply, the air was filled with a crescendo of shooting in the street at the front of the apartment. Rushing to the bedroom window they were in time to see people and uniformed police criss-crossing the road outside a bank, diving for shelter as the firing continued. The get-away car was attempting to escape through the police marksmen and swerved violently before disappearing down the first side street.

Alan Miles had been planning the raid for weeks and had assembled an experienced team of bank robbers. The strategy was simple. 3pm was the slackest time of the day and only two counter-staff would be manning the tills. With four raiders involved, two would be armed with strict orders not to fire. All four would enter the bank when a signal showed that there were no customers. One would man the door as lookout; the armed pair would frighten the staff and Alan would demand that his case should be filled quickly from the safe which always seemed to be unlocked with the door ajar. It was a well-tried plan.

But luck was not on their side. An additional member of staff who was on the public side of the counter, anticipated the purpose of the four men and screamed for the alarm to be pushed. One raider panicked and shot him dead. The others dived for the safety of the floor. Alan leap-frogged the counter and helped himself to a case full of notes from the open safe. The whole affair was over in twenty seconds but they were not prepared for the reception outside. Armed police who had been given a late tip-off were just arriving in two cars and the shooting began. Two raiders fell immediately whilst Alan and one other dived into their car. Both had been lucky but as they moved from the pavement Alan's companion was hit and fell across him, causing him to swerve but probably saved Alan from injury. He negotiated a left turn and a right, into a factory yard, where his second get-away car was parked.

Without any feelings for his mate who lay dying in the passenger seat, he casually picked up the case and drove away to a lay-by near his current one room flat, where he could remain undetected for as long as he wished. At no time had he divulged his own personal details to any of the team but he would be able to contact them if necessary. He opened a beer and turned on the wireless. Time could stand still. He was in no hurry.

An hour later, his curiosity caused him to open the case to quantify his gains. He smiled to himself: the bank had done most of the calculations for him. Neat piles of notes were all facing the same way and different colour elastic bands for the £1 and ten shilling notes. How thoughtful! For the first time in his life he read the assurance on the notes that they were legal tender in all the Commonwealth countries. That would be fortunate, as one of his favoured options would be to take a ship to England and escape the never-ending depression in Australia. His mind turned to the possibility that he may be the only survivor of the raid, removing any needs for share-outs. Why hadn't the wireless broadcast a report of the raid? His stomach turned over at the thought of leaving Bert dying and he had to call out loud to pull himself together.

At the age of nineteen this had been his third bank raid and his last. It was now time to plan the next phase of turning his ill-gotten gains into a soft life and the only way to achieve that would be to go to England, far away from prying eyes and the fears of strangers knocking on the door. Patience would be paramount. He must be prepared to lie low for four or five weeks, time enough for a beard and moustache to get established.

Suddenly, the announcer on the wireless blurted out the blood-curdling news. One bank staff and three raiders had died. Bert had dragged himself from the car which was now in the hands of the police and had been found lying in the yard, dead. Alan turned off the wireless and paced the room, coming to grips with the reality of being a number one target of the police and the community.

The following day brought the reality of his predicament. Whilst risking an early morning attempt to buy a bottle of milk, he was faced with a poster in the dairy window, offering a reward for this man. He would have to get used to drinking tea without milk.

Fate moves in strange ways. How could Charlotte, a hard-up young barmaid, have anticipated that March 1937 would have been the turning point of her life and that the driver of the brown Hillman saloon car drawing up outside The Brigadier Gerard, was about to drive into her life? She was sitting in the front garden enjoying a burst of spring sunshine. Even had she been an artist she couldn't possibly have expected to be able to draw such a perfect specimen of manhood. The tall slim young man who stepped from the car sported check plus fours, a high-necked, cable-stitched cardigan, was clean-shaven and had a flat cap matching the trousers.

"Good morning madam, Keith Burbridge. Does the Brigadier have a room for rent?"

His southern hemisphere accent enhanced his appearance.

"It does, sir, but there's a problem. The owner is seriously ill in hospital and his wife is at his bedside." But not wanting to end the meeting on an inconclusive note, she added quickly, "but I can show it to you."

"Are you the daughter of the house?"

"Oh no sir, but I have a big hand in running the place, especially since Mr. Spencer fell ill last year."

Mrs. Spencer had the worries of the manual side of the business taken from her, as the visitor willingly moved the barrels, restocked the shelves and tended the fire. Keith got a home at a reasonable rent and Charlotte enjoyed the pleasure of having young company throughout the day. The regulars in The Brigadier had fun imitating the southern accent and Keith was accepted all round the village. Fate was doing good turns for everyone. Gradually, the relationship between him and Charlotte blossomed and after a short engagement, they married in 1939. His wedding gift to her was the deeds of The Brigadier, having purchased it from the Spencers. Charlotte's response was to give herself freely on their wedding night, her first taste of such fruit.

Albert was born in February, 1940, the day on which Keith received papers from the Government calling him for military service. Amidst the tears Keith elected to join the Royal Air Force and after training as a spitfire pilot he transferred to the RAAF and posted to Biggin Hill where he survived The Battle of Britain. Towards the end of the war, after service in Italy and Germany, the Australians were back in Kent and Keith had more time to extend his love for Charlotte and Albert. On several occasions he brought other RAAF officers on leave, building up a friendship in the village for the Australians.

Many of the Aussie personnel were cricketers with top class clubs' experience and during the last few weeks of the war matches at near county standard were arranged. This lead to the formation of the Australian Services XI who were called upon to play five Test Matches with England starting less than two weeks after the end of the war. Keith volunteered to be baggage man for the team and following the fifth match he invited the team to play a friendly in

Horton Regis and be guests of the village. Thousands of people flocked to the match and many had no chance of seeing any action. But Keith made his name locally and on demobilisation, he was elected Chairman of the Parish Council.

His love for his family lead to their second son, Jack, arriving in June 1946. Keith's cup of joy was full to overflowing. Nobody could be happier. Ten years had seen him travel from the depths of the Australian depression to the ecstatic heights of being with the loveliest family in an appreciative arena. He was financially secure and his wartime experiences had made him a very selfless person.

Jenny and Brian spent nearly an hour at the cemetery, sad, but appreciative of the fact that somebody had been attending their son's grave. Winter pansies nodded their welcome as the couple approached and the epitaph of thanks from the local community brought Jenny to her knees with tears streaming down her cheeks.

"I'm so glad we came."

"So am I," added Brian. "We must try and find out who looks after Roger's grave."

Inside the church, Jenny found a Book of Remembrance and sure enough, an entry had been made, referring to Roger's generosity of coming from Australia and giving his life so that the villagers could live in peace.

Back in the Brigadier Gerard they were enjoying a warming hot toddy with Charlotte and relaying their pleasure of seeing the villagers' comments.

"Keith put the stone there," said Charlotte. "The two of them had flown together."

Suddenly, Brian noticed that the photographs of the cricket teams had been removed. Charlotte was equally surprised but found that the framed pictures were behind the bar. Brian's curiosity took over and he wracked his brains to try and remember where he had seen Keith's picture.

Charlotte casually mentioned the removal to Keith when he returned home and for the first time she saw the aggressive side of her husband.

"I thought that they ought to be presented in a better fashion," he shouted. "Is that a crime? Why all the fuss?"

"No fuss, darling, I think it's a good idea," she said, taking the heat out of the conversation. But the outburst left Brian confused.

"Miles! Miles! That was his name."

Jenny and Brian were half way across the Indian Ocean, homeward bound.

"Who's name? What are you talking about Brian?"

"The Sydney bank robber. You remember, 1936. We watched the raid from our window. The place was littered with the "Wanted" posters but they never found him. Now, I have! Think of that reward."

"Oh, I don't know. We are fortunate that Roger had such a good friend, Brian," replied Jenny.

"Yes, I suppose so. Let bygones ...."

WEAPON OF MASS DESTRUCTION

When I was a boy, the wireless was the medium for laughter. One of my favourite comedians was the "Odd Ode" man, Cyril Fletcher. He would tell a story in rhyme without deviating from the stereo-type composition of an Ode.
"Odd ode number one, pin back your lug holes …..This the tale of Gert and Mable, who bought themselves a dining table."
Whenever I hear an ode, I imagine Cyril reciting it.

I wanted to tell a tale about a firearm that had been selected for a story project and decided that the Odd Ode formula would catch the mood.

ODD ODE ON A WEAPON OF MASS DESTRUCTION

This is the tale of Gert and Mable who bought themselves a dining table.
T'was not the sort you'd see indoors adorning lounge or kitchen floors
Without the legs of Ann the Queen perhaps the smallest ever seen.
The measurement was two foot square and made for eating without chair
For clients who would come and go, fast food was all that they would know
The leg, this item had but one, not made for people having fun.
The six foot upright when in place with crossing members at the base
On level ground would stand erect and on the top one could detect
Four corner posts to hold aloof a gabled tar macadammed roof.
Yes, dear friends it sounds absurd, the table was for hungry bird.
Gert had paid a handsome fee to join a club RSPB
And all the pictures in their book convinced the pair that they should look
At families of the feathered kind devouring all that they could find.
They placed it on the kitchen lawn and covered it with bread and corn.
Two balls of fat to feed the tits, peanuts, seed and bacon bits.
With camera poised and picture book the girls prepared to sit and look
At first the birds seemed very shy and many of them just flew by.
But soon a pair of bluetits came, a bird that both the girls could name.
A Great tit, coal tit, chaffinch too, all fighting just like all birds do.
The finches too, both gold and green, prettiest birds they'd ever seen.
Then one morning came the jay and all the birds just flew away.
It's lazy hopping, beigey pink, a flash of blue and white distinct
Made Gert and Mable scream with joy. A bird so large but yet so coy.

But even more was on its way, a woodpecker had come to stay.
As Mable grasped the book of birds she noted the descriptive words
A bright red nape denotes a male with black and white on wings and tail.
With lots of white upon its tum and at the rear, a bright red bum.
Day after day the girls kept guard, noting points on each bird's card
In just a month, their records showed, a score of different types had glowed.
Then one day at early hour, Mable shouted, "Leave the shower
Take a look at what's outside," and Gert looked out and nearly cried
For lying there midst fur and fat were two black birds and next door's cat.
And Gert, displaying rage and hope, let out a yell and threw the soap.
It caught the midrift of the black, which cleared the fence without its snack.
No sooner was the moggy done, another rodent joined the fun.
"Look", cried Mabel, "there's a rat, let's have a stick to frighten that."
Gert took a look, was not amused to see the bird house get abused
"A squirrel grey, must be a male, it's just a rat with pretty tail".
No matter how the two girls tried, they couldn't budge the rat aside.
Ignoring clods of earth and sticks, the beast performed amazing tricks.
With rear toes clinging to the pole, the front ones reached the furthest goal
With torso stretched from head to toe, his tummy white and sex did show.
Now readers of the "Squirrel News" started coming, forming queues.
Not just the odd one here and there, but dozens, stealing all the fare.
Said Mabel, "Gert what shall we do? They've spoilt the fun for me and you".
Not speaking, Gert upstairs did run, returning with a pistol gun.
An automatic made in Rome, with 9 shots in its rusty dome
"My husband used this as a spy, he said, with this, ten men did die.

With 50m guarantee, you couldn't beat that accuracy."
"Have you ever fired that thing? I'm happier a stick to fling."
"Don't worry girl, I'll be alright," and got the squirrel in the sight.
The firing gave poor Gert a shock, but off the house the shot did knock
The unsuspecting squirrel grey, no more to fight another day.
"Well done, it's worked, the problems cease, now the birds can live in peace."
But squirrels came in by the score and Gert's new toy shot more and more
And wanting to enjoy the action, Mabel grasped the great attraction.
But lacking all the know-how skill she failed each time the rats to kill.
And in an act of desperation she turned to Gert with consternation
"There's something stuck, I'm fairly sure, I cannot get to fire no more."
And accidently pressed the trigger and Gert lay there, an inert figure.
The moral of this sorry verse "if things are bad they can get worse."
For Mabel, she's in prison still , unable to enjoy the thrill
Of all the pleasure that one gets by feeding birds and garden pets.

Printed in the United Kingdom by
Lightning Source UK Ltd., Milton Keynes
139231UK00001B/56/P